She was breaking Rule #1 of The Book According to Samantha Spade

Thou shalt not... No sooner did the thought occur to her than Jacquie's mind went blank and she surrendered to the magical play of Rick's hands on her body. He eased her back against a pile of flotation cushions and held her tight until the boat stopped rocking beneath them.

He unzipped her shorts and ever so carefully drew them down her legs until she was able to kick them off. The next thing to go was her vest, followed by her shoulder holster and shirt and finally, her pretty lace bra.

"Hold on tight," he whispered, stripping off his jeans and causing the boat to rock frantically. Little laps of water trickled over the side.

"Hurry!" she urged, her heated body crying out for release.

He entered her then, filling her body—her very soul—with his incredible strength and powerful thrusts. Even the dangerous movements of the boat couldn't compete with the quaking waves of ecstasy that washed over her.

Finally, when the boat stopped rocking and the world stopped spinning, she blew across his heated chest. "My aunt's going to kill me."

"Your aunt won't know."

"You don't know Aunt Samantha," she said. "She'll know."

Dear Reader,

I never thought I needed a bodyguard, but after seeing Kevin Costner play the part, hiring one is now on my "things to do" list, along with winning the lottery and learning to skate like Scott Hamilton.

What I want is a bodyguard to stand guard in front of the refrigerator, one who will refuse to budge no matter how much I beg, plead or threaten to throw myself on his mercy. I want someone to plow a path for me through the end-of-the-month sales and stare down anyone who tries to steal my parking space. Now, that would be heaven.

Of course, not all bodyguards are tall and handsome. Sometimes a bodyguard is a woman, and I have to admit, I'm tempted to send in my application. But as my husband pointed out, there isn't a big demand for bodyguards with flabby thighs. Oh well, we can't all be Kevin Costner.

Happy Reading!

Margaret Brownley

P.S. Don't miss Ruth Jean Dale's A PRIVATE EYEFUL, the December finale of Harlequin Temptation's HERO FOR HIRE miniseries.

BODY LANGUAGE
Margaret Brownley

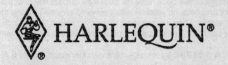

HARLEQUIN®

TORONTO • NEW YORK • LONDON
AMSTERDAM • PARIS • SYDNEY • HAMBURG
STOCKHOLM • ATHENS • TOKYO • MILAN • MADRID
PRAGUE • WARSAW • BUDAPEST • AUCKLAND

To Betty Duran (a.k.a. Ruth Jean Dale), who's charming,
funny and can be reached any time of day or night
during a crisis.
With friends like this, who needs a bodyguard?

ISBN 0-373-25805-4

BODY LANGUAGE

Copyright © 1998 by Margaret Brownley.

This edition published by arrangement with Harlequin Books S.A.

® and TM are trademarks of the publisher. Trademarks indicated with
® are registered in the United States Patent and Trademark Office, the
Canadian Trade Marks Office and in other countries.

Printed in U.S.A.

Prologue

JACQUIE SUMMERS KNEW from the word *go* that working for her aunt would be no picnic. But not until that Monday morning in early May, after sailing into her newly assigned office, did it really hit home: all those terrible rumors she'd heard about Samantha Spade might possibly be true.

Stopped dead in her tracks, Jacquie tried to convince herself that she had merely walked through the wrong door. Even if Aunt Samantha was as ruthless in business as the rumors implied, she wouldn't pull something like this on her very own niece, would she?

Jacquie ducked beneath a hanging feather duster for a better look at the nameplate on the desk. *Jack* Summers. That pretty much confirmed it. This *was* her office. "Aunt Samantha, how could you?"

Her aunt's protective service business was booming, and space in the three-story Victorian row house located in the most picturesque part of San Francisco was at a premium, but was it really necessary for Jacquie to share an office with the all-purpose cleaner?

While the other employees enjoyed a view of the Golden Gate Bridge and San Francisco Bay, Jacquie's office overlooked the cat run in back. Her aunt was testing her; she had to be.

Jacquie dropped her tote bag on the sturdy oak desk just as the telephone rang.

She had spent the past two months memorizing company policy as it was spelled out in *The Book According to Samantha Spade*. The number of dos and don'ts regarding telephone etiquette alone were staggering.

Determined to prove herself to her aunt, Jacquie threw one leg over a metal pail, sent a squeegee mop flying against the window, knocked a can of brass polish off a shelf and grabbed the phone on the second ring, as per rule number one. She would follow each and every one of her aunt's blasted commandments if it killed her.

"Hello...uh, S. J. Spade Insurance Agency. May I help you?" The insurance company was a front to protect Samantha's clients. The only insurance the company sold was bodily protection.

Her aunt Samantha's deep, no-nonsense voice boomed in her ear. "So what do you think of the office, Precious?"

Teetering on the high heels she'd worn to impress her aunt, her straight woolen skirt stretched to the limit, Jacquie straddled the metal pail and bit back the urge to tell her what she really thought.

"Well?" her aunt persisted.

"I *love* it," Jacquie said, determined to prove she could take whatever Samantha dished out. Besides, it wasn't all that bad. If it weren't for the brooms in the corners, the cleaning supplies and feather dusters, no one would ever guess she was sharing space with Mr. Euclid, the janitor.

Mr. Euclid was the only one in her aunt's employ who insisted upon and was granted the right to be addressed formally. Everyone else went by their first name.

"You do?" Her aunt seldom if ever revealed her innermost feelings, except, perhaps, when it suited her purposes, but she sounded just a tad surprised.

Jacquie grinned. Her aunt had always been her idol, her role model. What with a series of false career starts behind her, Jacquie had not done much to earn her aunt's approval in recent years, but that was about to change. She was determined to become the best bodyguard S. J. Spade Insurance had to offer. "It's perfect."

With some work, she might even convince herself that sharing space with a squeegee mop was a step up in the world.

"Now aren't you happy you came to work for me?"

Happy wasn't exactly the word that came to mind. *Desperate* was more like it. After two years of law school, she had finally accepted the inevitable and dropped out; she could never follow in her father's footsteps.

"One year, Aunt Samantha. I've agreed to work for you for one year and not a day longer."

"Trust me, Precious, it will be the best year of your life. You won't have a thing to squawk about. You wait and see. In the end, you'll thank me."

Jacquie moved the pail aside and slid a slender hip onto the edge of the desk. "And don't think I'm going to give up my idea of opening a detective agency." She hoped to save enough money by the end of the year to do exactly that.

"A niece of mine give up? Never!"

Jacquie chewed on her lower lip. "I gave up law school." Not to mention business school, travel school and the Culinary Institute of San Francisco.

"That's because your heart wasn't in it. You thought going to law school would please your father."

It had, too, as long as she agreed to stay away from criminal law. Unfortunately, she didn't have the heart for corporate law, or even family law.

"Nothing short of you checking yourself into a convent would please that man," Samantha concluded.

Jacquie felt as if a weight had been lifted off her shoulders. It was bad enough disappointing her father, but she hated to think she'd disappointed her aunt, too. "Then you don't disapprove of my plans?"

"Of course not. I like the idea of you having your own agency. But I'll feel a lot better if you have some business smarts to go along with those big plans of yours. That's what I'm going to teach you, Precious—how to run a business."

"I know how to run a business, Aunt Samantha. Remember? Before I went to law school, I took two years of business." Another bad idea.

"Don't remind me. I only hope that a year is enough time to repair the damage."

Jacquie decided not to debate the issue. Besides, it wouldn't do any good. Once her aunt's mind was made up, even a sledgehammer couldn't change it. Jacquie picked up her ID badge. It matched her nameplate. "By the way, my badge is wrong."

"Wrong? Wrong? How could it be wrong? I checked it myself."

"It says Jack instead of Jacquie. *Jack* Summers."

"Of course it says Jack. You're a bodyguard, not a fashion model. Jack is a good solid name. It'll give clients confidence in your abilities."

"You insist upon being called by your full name, Samantha. Well, I feel the same way about my name."

"No you don't, or you'd be called Jacqueline."

"But—"

"Trust me on this, Jacquie," her aunt said in that don't-talk-while-I'm-interrupting tone of hers. "I know what I'm talking about. Mark will fill you in on your first assignment." Mark Spenser was her aunt's right-hand man, but some called him a saint for putting up with Samantha's eccentric ways. "Any questions?"

"Not a one. Thank you for calling, Aunt *Sam.*"

Smiling to herself, Jacquie carefully placed the handset into its cradle. She took off her suit jacket and draped it across the back of the chair. Not once in all her twenty-six years had she ever had the nerve to call her aunt anything but Samantha. Until today.

She picked up her ID badge and pinned it to the front of her white tailored blouse. Apparently the name Jack was having an effect on her already. Either that or the strong smell of disinfectant had triggered a gene for boldness previously buried in her Viking roots.

With a sense of purpose, she pushed the bottles of window cleaners to one side and set her tote on a shelf next to her desk. She then kicked off her high heels. How in the world did her aunt walk around all day in spike-heeled shoes?

A tap sounded at the door and *Saint* Mark walked in, wrinkling his nose and waving his hand in front of his face. "Oh, dear. It smells awful in here. Just awful."

Jacquie couldn't agree more. "Think of it as a pine forest."

The boyish look on Mark's face matched the grinning faces on his Mickey Mouse tie. "Welcome to the S. J. Spade Insurance Agency, where nothing is what it seems." He dropped a file folder on Jacquie's desk. "Your first assignment as a bodyguard," he announced. "You've heard of Mrs. Edward J. Ballinger III, haven't you?"

"Yes, of course." The elderly widow was one of San Francisco's wealthiest women. Jacquie's spirits rose. Maybe her aunt meant what she said about letting Jacquie take on meaningful assignments that would allow her to utilize her varied talents.

"She wants protection for Lord Byron. It seems someone is trying to kidnap him."

"Really? How awful." *A lord? I'm going to protect a lord! Well, what do you know?* Her first day on the job and already she had been assigned to protect a *titled* person. Aunt Samantha obviously had more confidence in her than Jacquie had ever dreamed, and she would not let her down.

Mark's face grew serious. "Are you sure you're up to this?"

"Of course I'm up to it," Jacquie said. Drawing both hands level with her shoulders, she sliced the air with a karate chop, letting out a loud *"Kiai."*

One didn't grow up with three brothers without learning survival skills. Out of necessity, she'd learned how to deliver a quick blow, a mean flip and even a disabling hold. This had proved to be a blessing recently when a stranger tried to mug her. The man had looked positively dazed as the police hauled him away. Even her brother Kyle was impressed.

"Martial arts, fencing, sharpshooting, archery. You name it, it's mine," she said, making no attempt at modesty.

She'd also spent six grueling weeks at the body-guard boot camp her aunt required all prospective employees to attend, and Jacquie had the bruises to prove it. She gave Mark a half smile. "If all else fails, I can even whip up a mean soufflé."

Mark looked interested. "Ah, yes, your aunt told me you attended cooking school. You don't happen to have a good recipe for beef Wellington, do you?"

"The best. But I'm sorry. I don't give out my secret recipes."

Mark looked disappointed, but he took it philosophically. "Oh, well, if you ever change your mind." Two vertical lines appeared between his eyebrows. "Tell me, what do you know about dogs?"

"Dogs?" Jacquie lowered herself into her chair. She suddenly had a very bad premonition. "Why do you ask?"

Mark turned and headed for the door. "Lord Byron is a poodle, and like I said, someone is trying to kidnap him."

1

Three months later

RICK WESTLEY STEPPED OVER the poster partly buried beneath his overturned desk. Sex Is the Most Fun You Can Have without Laughing.

The last time he'd seen that particular poster, it was hanging over the watercooler in the employees' lounge. Now the lounge was gone. So, for that matter, was his office, or at least two sides of it. The bomb had blasted through the outer wall of the brick building, leaving an unprecedented view of the parking lot.

He was lucky the explosion hadn't destroyed the entire Stanwicke and Lanswell Software Corporation, where he worked. Hell, he was lucky to be alive.

A frizzy-haired man with a walkie-talkie stepped over a pile of rubble. The yellow letters on the back of his dark jacket identified him as an FBI agent. Behind him a uniformed policeman stood guard.

The place swarmed with emergency crews. Firemen, ambulance workers and members of the bomb squad surged through the building and parking lot. Police shouted warnings to onlookers straining against the yellow tape barrier, trying to see around reporters.

The air vibrated with the low, throbbing sound of helicopters battling for space overhead.

After being checked by paramedics for possible injuries and given a clean bill of health, Rick had been granted permission to return to his office to retrieve his attaché case. So far, he'd found only the leather handle.

Anything of value, even his laptop computer, was buried beneath the rubble.

His friend and co-worker, Leonard "Lenny" Turner, ducked through the gaping hole in the brick wall and stepped over the remains of a filing cabinet.

Lenny mopped his dust-covered face with a handkerchief, his ginger hair damp with sweat. The Bay Area was in the midst of a heat wave. Due to the sweltering heat, the dust from the blast and a strange acrid smell, breathing was a chore.

"Whoo-ee," Lenny said. "It's a wonder we weren't both killed."

Rick turned over the wastebasket and pushed aside a chair. Still no attaché case. "How did you know?" he asked. All he could remember with any real clarity was opening his mail. Then, suddenly, Lenny had lunged across the room, snatched a package out of his hands and tossed it into the hall. The next thing Rick knew, he was on the floor.

Lenny had performed an amazing feat of bravery, especially given his physique. Lenny was no superhero, more paunchy than muscular and scarcely over five feet tall. It wasn't like him to move that fast—unless a woman was involved.

"How did you know about the bomb?"

Lenny leaned against the overturned desk. "The package ticked." He faked an Italian accent and shook his cupped hand in front of Rick's face. "How many times I gotta tell you, mail don't tick."

Rick couldn't help but laugh. Lenny had always been a clown, even back in grammar school where they'd first met. "I'll remember that." The package had been wrapped in plain brown paper, with no return address. Still, he'd had no reason to believe the package posed a threat. Not until he pulled that cord. "So what are you doing here today?"

"I promised my kid I would talk to his class on Monday morning. It's Career Day at his summer day camp. I stopped by to pick up some parts. Thought the kids would get a kick out of seeing what the inside of a computer looks like."

"You saved my life."

Lenny grinned. "You know what that means, don't you? You owe me."

Rick draped his arm around Lenny's shoulders. "You name it, it's yours, pal," he said, grinning back. "Let's get out of here."

Outside, TV reporters attacked everyone in sight with microphones and minicams. Lenny waved the mikes out of Rick's face as the two of them hurried to the parking lot. "Damn, they're like vultures," Lenny muttered.

FBI agent Kent Harrison chased after them. "Mr. Westley! I'd like to ask you a few questions."

"You go on," Lenny said. "I've already told him everything I know and it's my turn to take Jimmy to his Little League game." Lenny shared custody of his son with his ex-wife, Janet.

"See you," Rick said. "And Lenny...thanks." Rick had never felt at such a loss for words. How do you thank someone for saving your life?

"Sure thing." Lenny gave him a playful punch in the arm. "Do me a favor. From now on, *do* look a gift horse in the mouth."

"I'll remember that. And good luck on Career Day."

Lenny walked off and Rick turned toward the FBI agent. He seldom if ever drank, but he would have given anything for a stiff drink right about now. "Blast away," he said, then quickly added, "figuratively speaking, of course."

Agent Harrison stared at Rick through his dark glasses, his face void of expression. "Did you notice anything unusual about the package in question?"

"No, nothing. I thought it was one of the books I ordered."

"So the package was the size of a book?"

"Yeah, with one of those plastic zip cords."

"Did it come with the regular mail?"

Rick thought for a moment, but his head throbbed and it was difficult to concentrate. "I think so. I left work early yesterday, before the mail came. So naturally, when I saw the stack of mail on my desk this morning, I assumed it had been delivered with the regular mail."

"And what time was that?"

"Around ten, ten-thirty."

"Do you generally open your own mail?"

"Yes, always."

"Is Saturday your usual workday?"

"I usually work at home on Saturdays. But I needed a backup disk I'd left at the office. So I stopped by to pick it up."

"How long were you here before the bomb went off?"

"Maybe ten, fifteen minutes tops. I checked my voice mail and E-mail first, before checking my regular mail."

"And you noticed nothing out of the ordinary prior to the bomb blast?"

Rick squeezed his eyes shut and forced himself to relive the moments leading up to the blast. "Let's see. I started to pull the cord, but I heard a hissing sound and stopped. I remember seeing white smoke coming from the side of the package and a smell. Yeah, it's coming back to me. I remember the strange smell."

Harrison asked a few more questions before handing him a business card. "If you think of anything else, give me a call."

"Sure thing." Rick started across the parking lot toward his red Chevy Blazer. He found what was left of his empty attaché case on the hood of his car. The case had left a dent the size of a soup can on his year-old vehicle, but otherwise, his car had escaped any major damage.

He glanced back at the damaged building and shook his head in disbelief. Suddenly, it hit him just how lucky he was.

He tossed the leather case into a gaping trash bin and opened the door to the driver's side.

"One more question, Mr. Westley."

Rick leveled his gaze across the roof of his car to where the FBI agent stood watching him.

"Can you think of a reason why someone might want to see you dead?"

"Dead?" Lorraine Heathrow came rushing to his side. "Someone wants to see you dead?"

Rick hardly recognized the office manager. He'd never seen Lorraine when she didn't look immaculate, every silver hair in place. Today she was a wreck. Her hair looked as if it had been styled with an eggbeater.

Instead of her usual trim business suit, she wore white shorts, a San Francisco Giants T-shirt and a pair of slippers shaped like Dalmatian dogs.

"No one wants to see me dead," Rick said. "And what are you doing here? It's your day off."

"I came as soon as I heard about the blast on the news." Lorraine turned to Harrison. "Do you really think someone is trying to kill him?"

"That's usually why people send mail bombs." One of the other FBI agents called to Harrison from inside the building. Harrison waved to the agent, then hurried off to join him.

Rick cupped Lorraine's elbow and led her back to her car. He had never seen her look so upset or shaken and he was worried. A sweet-natured woman in her early sixties, she had recently been treated for a minor heart problem and was under doctor's orders to avoid stress.

"Go home, Lorraine." He opened her car door. "There's nothing you can do here."

"This is serious, Rick. You could have been killed."

"But I wasn't. And now that we know some crackpot's on the loose, we'll take precautions."

Relief crossed her face. "Does that mean you're going to hire a bodyguard?"

The idea hadn't even occurred to him. "A what? I don't need a bodyguard."

"Well, of course you do. You heard what that FBI agent said." She dug in her purse. "Here. Take this." She handed him a business card. "It's the best bodyguard agency in the Bay Area. All the important people use their services."

Rick stared at the card in his hand. "It says 'insurance agency.'"

"That's just a cover. It's really a *protective* service agency. You know how things are today. You can't call a spade a spade, or a bodyguard a bodyguard." She tossed her purse onto the passenger seat and slid behind the steering wheel. "Mention my name."

With his hand resting on the door frame, Rick lowered his head. "How come you know so much about this bodyguard agency?"

"I know the owner, Samantha Spade. We met when we were the same age. Now she claims she's ten years younger."

"And you think I should trust her with my life?"

"I wouldn't have suggested it if I didn't think so. Just don't ask her to do any math problems."

Rick grinned. "Anything you say, boss."

Normally, Lorraine laughed when he referred to her as boss. Today, he failed to coax so much as a smile from her. "Promise me you'll call her."

"I'll think about it." Rick straightened and slammed the door shut. Stepping away from the car, he watched Lorraine mouth "call her" before she drove by him and disappeared into the sea of reporters and flashing cameras.

He took one last look of disbelief at the building and shook his head. Who in hell would want to see him dead?

JACQUIE SUMMERS WOULD BE dead—or at least her career as a bodyguard would be—if she didn't reach her client's cabin soon. Already she was three hours behind schedule. Nothing confused her more than road maps, and this particular one took the cake. She couldn't make heads nor tails out of it.

After the fiasco with that spoiled pooch Lord Byron, she didn't dare mess up another job. Whatever this assignment entailed, it couldn't be half as bad as the last one. Never had she seen Aunt Samantha so angry. And all because that snooty dog with the imposing name had been kidnapped from right beneath Jacquie's very nose. Not to mention that Lord Byron was the first client her aunt's company had lost during all its years in business. Mrs. Edward J. Ballinger III already had her lawyers working on the case, and a lawsuit was almost certain.

It was a wonder Jacquie's aunt hadn't fired her on the spot.

She steered the car around a large boulder that had slid down the mountainside, Samantha's angry voice still ringing in her ears. Not that Jacquie blamed her aunt, of course; she had every reason to be upset.

Jacquie still couldn't believe it herself. For three solid months, she'd not let Lord Byron out of her sight. She'd slept with him, taken her meals with him, watched him like a hawk. But it wasn't easy to save a dog with raging hormones.

Lord Byron's lusty appetite had gotten him into trouble with every neighbor within a five-mile radius. Mrs. Ballinger refused to have the dog fixed, claiming it was unnatural, and, besides, he was prime breeding stock.

Not even a ten-foot fence could keep the four-legged Don Juan from populating the area with curly haired litters. As it turned out, nor could a bodyguard, no matter how vigilant. Jacquie had almost killed herself chasing after him and pulling him away from some sweet canine miss.

Holding the map across her steering wheel, she kept one eye on the narrow dirt road that twisted and turned through woods so thick virtually no sunlight penetrated. At one point the trees on either side formed an arch, blocking out the sky altogether.

She took a bite out of a sandwich and grimaced. Who in their right mind would surround a cucumber with two slices of bread and call it a sandwich?

This was absolutely the last time she'd ever let her landlady pack her lunch.

All right, so she'd accepted her aunt's job offer out of guilt. But now her pride was at stake. Her aunt had trusted her with an important client and she had failed miserably.

Though she doubted she could ever redeem herself in the eyes of the animal activists who threatened to picket her aunt's agency, Jacquie was determined to regain Samantha's trust.

And if that meant playing nursemaid to some fool living on a remote mountain with no paved roads and, as far as she could tell, not so much as a single signpost to point the way, then that's what she would do.

She tossed the map aside. Dotted lines, nothing but dotted lines. By the looks of things, she had to travel another twelve miles or so of dirt road before reaching her destination.

It was closer to fifteen miles before she spotted the lake through the woods. Following the directions Mark had given her, she took the right fork, then made a sharp left.

The cabin was almost hidden by a thick growth of trees. Had she blinked, she would have missed it. She followed the narrow road that circled behind the cabin and parked her car next to the red Blazer.

It felt good to climb out of the front seat and stretch her legs. It had taken her nearly six-and-a-half hours to make the drive from San Francisco to Falcon Heights, a sleepy little skiing village nestled in the Sierras, and another hour and a half to find the cabin.

The road was so rutted in places she had been forced to crawl along at little more than five miles an hour.

She grabbed her duffel bag and a sweatshirt from the trunk. Already the air felt cool, and she was dressed in shorts.

She flung her bag over her shoulder and started toward the cabin.

"Hold it right there."

Startled by the rough male voice, Jacquie stopped dead in her tracks.

2

"TURN AROUND."

This time the voice sounded more assertive than rough, and mildly threatening. Jacquie decided that arguing with its owner was probably not a good idea. Especially when it was possible the man held a gun, maybe even a rifle, pointed straight at her.

She turned, but all she could see through the thick growth were two handsomely tooled cowboy boots.

Aunt Samantha's words came back to taunt her. *You mess up this job and you're history.*

"Nice boots," she called, hoping to get the man to show his face.

"What do you want?" The voice was gruff this time, more insistent.

"I'm looking for Rick Westley."

The bushes shook and suddenly she found herself staring into eyes as blue as the clear mountain lake that shimmered through the trees.

She'd guessed wrong about the rifle; he was carrying a bucket filled with kindling. As far as she could tell, the man was unarmed, though his killer good looks surely counted as a weapon of sorts. One look at his handsome face and she was ready to surrender to him without a fight—something she would never do had he been armed with only a gun.

He glanced at her duffel bag before his gaze collided with hers. "I'm Rick Westley. Who are you?"

Sighing with relief, she dropped the canvas bag to the ground. "I'm Jack Summers."

His eyes widened in disbelief. "*You're* Jack Summers?"

"Yes," she said. It wasn't often that she felt self-conscious beneath a man's scrutiny, but this wasn't any ordinary Joe. This man was drop-dead gorgeous.

His gaze took a dive, lingering momentarily on her tanned legs and open-toed sandals, before traveling up to her auburn hair. She didn't need a psychic to know what he was thinking.

She stood little more than five foot three, and she was probably the only woman alive who claimed to weigh ten pounds more than she actually did.

"You gotta be kidding."

His surprise she could tolerate, but now he was getting downright insulting. She lifted her chin and looked him square in the eye. "I'm a well-trained, professional bodyguard."

He didn't exactly laugh, but his mouth certainly quirked upward, revealing a flash of even white teeth. "Next you'll be telling me you're trained in martial arts."

"It's true," she said. "Not only am I proficient in a variety of martial arts, I'm an expert marksman." She decided not to mention her soufflé-making skills.

He moved closer and the musky smell of his aftershave taunted her feminine senses.

Though *The Book According to Samantha Spade* made no mention of body parts, she would bet that staring at his powerful jean-clad thighs was strictly forbidden. For that reason, she tore her gaze away. It wasn't easy, but acting professional under pressure wasn't meant to be. Of course, once her attention settled on his handsome square face, she had no trouble keeping it there.

He had a straight nose, a full sensuous mouth and a cleft in his chin that offered an intriguing contrast to an otherwise unyielding jaw. His brown hair was thick and wavy and, judging by the lock that fell carelessly across his forehead, had a mind of its own. The wayward strands gave her an odd sense of satisfaction; Mr. Westley might think he was in control, but obviously he was not!

She stood at attention as he circled her, and tried to recall which of her aunt's rules were relevant to the present situation. Other than *Thou shalt not lust after clients*, she couldn't think of a single one.

He stroked his chin, his dark brows slanting in a frown, and the reason was obvious. Even when she was standing tall, her head barely reached his broad shoulders.

"By martial arts, do you mean karate and kick-boxing? That kind of thing?" he asked.

She met his disbelieving eyes. "Would you care for a demonstration?"

"I'll take your word for it." Disbelief gave way

to amusement, and the look on his face was down-right patronizing!

She bit back the urge to smack that knowing smile off his handsome face and flip him to the ground, just as she had done to that annoying mugger on Market Street. Let the know-it-all make fun of her while lying flat on his back!

"You're in good hands with me," she said coolly. All right, so she'd lost Lord Byron. She was still a capable bodyguard, no matter what anyone said. But just to be on the safe side, she decided it wouldn't hurt to know exactly what she was getting herself into.

"I trust no one's tried to kidnap you?" She knew about the bomb, of course, but something could have happened in the last day or so that had not yet shown up in his file. Besides, with his sexy good looks, Rick Westley could be just as much of a threat to the neighbors as Lord Byron.

"No, they're trying to blow me up."

She sighed in relief. At least he wouldn't be roaming the streets at night. "Thank God. I mean…then there's been no other attempt on your life?"

"None."

"I guarantee you have nothing to worry about with me around."

She surveyed the lay of the land. She'd spoken with more confidence than was prudent. The isolated cabin, located off a narrow dirt road not fit for a mule, was a bodyguard's nightmare, but it was only part of the overall security problem. Her work was cut out for her.

"I'm afraid things aren't quite that simple," he said. "I don't know how to put this to you other than to come right out and say it. You're fired."

Surprised by the abrupt dismissal, she tore her gaze away from the thick woods behind the cabin and stared at him, openmouthed. "F-fired?" she stuttered.

"It's nothing personal," he said, looking apologetic. "I asked for a bodyguard."

"I *am* a bodyguard," she said firmly. "And I consider being fired very personal."

"What I meant to say is…I'm sure you're a very good bodyguard, you're just not the right one for me." His courteous manner did not hide his patronizing tone. "If somebody really is out to kill me, then I want a bodyguard who's six foot six and weighs at least three hundred pounds. I don't need some featherweight following me around. I'm sure you understand?"

She regarded him with an icy stare. "Perfectly."

"I'm sorry…" He glanced around as if trying to figure out something more to say to her. He then shrugged and started toward the cabin.

"Watch it," she said. She reached beneath her vest and rested her hand on her gun.

He swung around. "What?"

"We're at our most vulnerable at our own front doors," she explained. Her back toward him, she scanned the surrounding area. "Think Lennon."

"John Lennon? The Beatles?"

She chanced a sideways glance at him. "Right at his own front door. From now on, never leave by the same door twice. Next time use the back door."

"I don't have a back door," he said.

She spun around to face him. "Are you trying to get yourself killed? An isolated cabin. A dirt road. A single door. A car left out in the open where anyone and his brother can get to it. This cabin is an assassin's paradise."

He looked at her as if she was speaking a foreign language. "Listen, I'm not even sure someone *is* trying to kill me. My boss insisted upon hiring a bodyguard and I finally agreed, in order to get him and my officer manager off my back. I really don't need a bodyguard."

"It's your call, mister."

"Yeah, well…" He hesitated. "It's, uh…too late for you to start back down the mountain. You can stay the night, if you like. There's a guest room upstairs. I'll pay you for your trouble, of course." Without giving her a chance to reply, he turned, walked up the steps leading to the porch and vanished inside the cabin.

Hands on her hips, Jacquie glowered after him. No matter what excuses he made, he had fired her, clean and simple. He hadn't even give her a chance to prove herself.

For two cents, she'd turn around and head back to San Francisco, even if it meant coming face-to-face with those animal activists picketing her aunt's place of business. If Jacquie wasn't so practical, that's exactly what she would do. But the sun would soon disappear behind the mountains, and the thought of driving that narrow dirt road at night filled her with dread.

Like it or not, she was stuck till morning.

3

INSIDE THE CABIN, Rick flipped on the light switch and set the bucket of kindling on the hearth. It had been one of those days. Hell, it had been one of those weeks, starting with the bomb blast.

The cabin belonged to his boss, Russ Parker. Parker sure wasn't kidding when he'd said the place hadn't been used in over a year. Rick and Russ were two of a kind: they were both card-carrying, type-A workaholics.

The trait had ruined two marriages for Russ and had put a damper on any social life for Rick, but neither he nor Russ could seem to help themselves.

As far as Rick was concerned, the scenery that surrounded the cabin was secondary to the peace and quiet that would allow him to work undisturbed.

He'd not given the lake or the rugged mountains more than a passing glance since arriving at the cabin. He also liked the fact that the cabin didn't have a phone. At last he could get some real work done, with no interruptions. Maybe moving out here wasn't such a bad idea after all.

The cabin had been built from hand-hewed cedar logs by Parker's grandfather. With two bedrooms, a bathroom and a small but complete kitchen and dining alcove, the cabin was rustic, but comfortable. The big stone fireplace dominating an entire wall of the living room was not only practical but homey.

Russ had warned him about the comfortable overstuffed furniture, saying it was more conducive to curling up with a book or taking a nap than getting any real work done.

Parker's advice to Rick was to stay off the couch and keep the draperies closed to hide the sweeping view of the lake, mountains and woods.

Actually, the couch did look inviting. It had been a long day, or maybe it was simply the accumulation of stress that was catching up to him. Whatever it was, he was having a hard time thinking about work.

He had left San Francisco at dawn, arriving at the cabin before noon. The trip meant losing yet another day of work, but it wasn't as if he had a choice. His boss had insisted that Rick stay away from the temporary headquarters Stanwicke and Lanswell had taken over while construction workers repaired the bomb damage done to the old building.

Parker even made him move out of his own apartment until the FBI had tracked down the bomber, and for the last couple of nights, Rick had stayed at a downtown hotel.

But Parker made it clear the company would not be responsible for Rick's safety unless he left town altogether and kept his whereabouts secret from everyone, including his very own mother.

It had taken Rick the remainder of the afternoon

to air out the place, figure out how to work the generator and prepare the upstairs loft for the bodyguard.

He shook his head. Little did he know that the protection agency would send a woman. Not just a woman, but a half-pint.

What a pity. If it weren't for her size, she would probably be a formidable foe. Just thinking of the expression on her face—all big blue eyes and indignant scowls—made him chuckle.

Maybe it was just as well. He really did question the need for a bodyguard. The more he thought about it, the more convinced he was the bomb had been a fluke. Probably the work of some disgruntled ex-employee, who had sent the bomb to the office to create havoc, and had never meant to target any one person.

Rick couldn't imagine anyone wanting to kill him, personally. What could anyone hope to gain by seeing him dead?

He was a software engineer, for crissakes. A programmer. People didn't generally go around killing off *computer programmers!* Not even his current project could, by any stretch of the imagination, pose a threat to anyone.

He was working on a program that would permit computer software programs to "talk" to one another, regardless of name brands. His program would have a negative impact on big companies, as it would allow consumers to mix and match software to their hearts' content.

Granted, millions—perhaps billions—of dollars were at stake. It was the kind of project that might attract corporate spies, which was why he had been forced to keep the project under wraps. But murderers?

No, he didn't need a bodyguard, and he certainly didn't need a blue-eyed beauty distracting him from his work.

The bomb had put him three weeks behind schedule and that hurt. This latest setback was one in a series of delays that had plagued the project from the start. If he didn't know better, he'd think he was jinxed. Not that anything of major concern had happened until the bomb, just little nuisances that kept cropping up and putting him ever further behind.

First, a computer virus had wiped out his files, and soon after, his laptop had disappeared from his car. Next, electrical problems had popped up, requiring the company to rewire the entire building even though the original wiring was less than five years old.

Next, he'd suffered a bout of food poisoning that had landed him in the hospital for three days and made him swear off fast-food restaurants forever.

He had, at most, thirty days left to work out the bugs that still remained in his program. Otherwise, he didn't have a chance in hell of meeting Parker's production schedule. This time, nothing must go wrong.

Curious as to whether or not the female bodyguard would take him up on his offer to spend the night, he peered out the window.

Well, what do you know?

Two cardboard boxes were stacked next to her duffel bag. Standing so as not to be seen, he let his gaze roam lazily down the length of her.

Curved hips flared from a slender waist and tapered down to her shapely tanned legs. A knit top the exact shade of blue as her eyes molded her soft, rounded breasts.

Even from this distance he could see her pleasing mouth and cute upturned nose. Her short auburn hair hugged her pretty, heart-shaped face, and she moved with a spritely grace that was surprising, given her profession and the fact that she carried a gun and obviously knew how to use it.

Never in a million years would he have guessed she was a bodyguard. Not on sight alone. He'd have guessed a dancer, perhaps, with those legs. But not a bodyguard.

Though Parker had feared Rick would find the panoramic view of lake and mountains distracting, he was wrong. Rick had eyes only for the lady bodyguard.

She moved out of sight, and he eyed the pile of her belongings next to her car. How could someone so small require so much stuff?

His gaze lit on her again the moment she walked into view. He drew back when she glanced toward the cabin, but even from this distance he could see her eyes flash with impatience or anger, perhaps both. Well, who could blame her? He regretted having been so brusque with her earlier. None of this was her fault.

He heaved a deep sigh and pinched his forehead. The pressure of trying to complete this software program, coupled with the hair-raising experience of nearly having been blown to kingdom come, was taking its toll. The lady was due an apology. And maybe more...

Smiling to himself, he moved away from the window and turned toward the fireplace.

Earlier, he had arranged the logs and newspaper on the grate. Now he jammed a few pieces of kindling into place, then struck a match. He touched the flame to the paper and pulled back.

Already the air had turned chilly, and once the sun disappeared behind the mountains, the temperature would drop even more. Actually, he didn't mind the cool temperatures, but his guest didn't have much meat on those delicate bones of hers. Though what she did have was packed in all the right places.

The woman was tenacious, he'd give her that much. He doubted many people would travel nearly twenty miles on a rutted dirt road, even for pay, especially given Falcon Heights' geological unrest in recent years.

Flames leaped up and the kindling crackled. He drew away from the circle of warmth and stood. He started across the room, intent upon giving his guest a helping hand. But before he had a chance, the front door was flung open, and Jack came staggering into the cabin loaded down with her cardboard cartons and duffel bag.

No sooner had she stepped foot into the room than she tripped over the colorful rag rug. Making a superhuman effort to juggle her belongings, she did a slow dance, bumping up against an end table and sending the only lamp in the room flying.

"Holy smokes!" He grabbed the lamp just before it hit the floor, then whirled around to help her, but it was too late. Already, his blue-eyed guest had landed in a heap, the contents of the boxes scattered all around her.

He hurried to her side and pulled the canvas bag away from her bare legs. "Are you all right?" he asked, lifting a cardboard box off her chest.

She eyed him cautiously. "Yes, thank you."

He looked around for a place to set the box. A small metal container slid to the floor, the lid springing open. Its contents spilled across the rug. Rick stared, his mouth open.

Condoms! The box was filled with condoms and at least a dozen more were scattered around his feet.

Not bothering to hide his surprise, he lifted his eyes to stare at Jack, his eyebrows arched. "It never occurred to me that a bodyguard's duties were so...varied."

Her cheeks turned a pretty red. "I was told I'd be roughing it," she explained.

"Roughing it, huh?" He set the box on the leather couch. "I'd say you're prepared to deal with whatever nature has to offer."

Jack scrambled about the floor on hands and knees, offering Rick an intriguing view of her soft, rounded fanny. The hem of her shorts crept upward, revealing the little crease that separated her buttocks from her thighs. Now *that* was enough to distract a man, big time!

Unlike Parker, Rick found neither the furniture nor the view a liability, but the lady bodyguard—now that was whole different enchilada. Thank God she was only a temporary distraction.

She quickly scooped up the condoms, tossing them back into the tin box like so many pieces of candy. "It's my survival kit. A person can survive in the wilderness for days with these supplies."

"I bet," he said evenly. Pushing air through his lips, he stooped to help her.

Her eyes blazed with annoyance. "Well, they can. During the Vietnam War, my father's helicopter crashed into shark-infested waters and these—" she shook a foil-wrapped condom in his face "—saved his life. They make great tourniquets and come in handy when stabilizing broken legs."

"What do you know?" he drawled. She looked so serious, he couldn't resist teasing her. "You really can use them for every *conceivable* situation."

She gave him an odd look, as if she didn't know whether or not to take him seriously. "Yes, well…" She tossed the last of the condoms into her survival kit and snapped the lid shut. "Where do you want me to sleep?"

He straightened and nodded to the stairs leading to the loft. "You'll find everything you need up there," he said, his gaze never leaving her face. "I'm afraid there's only one bathroom." He pointed to the door behind the staircase. "Listen…" He shoved his hands in his pockets. "I know I was rough with you outside, but it's nothing to do with you personally. I've simply changed my mind. I don't need a bodyguard."

She regarded him warily. "Like I said, it's your call, mister."

"Rick. Call me Rick."

"Yeah, well…would you mind standing away from the window?"

"What?"

She pushed him out of the way, the pressure of her hand practically burning a hole through the flannel sleeve of his shirt. She then yanked the draperies closed. "You need to move your desk to the other side of the room." Before he had a chance to argue, she was already dragging the oak desk across the wooden floor to the blank wall on the far side of the room.

Rushing to help her, he grabbed hold of the opposite side of the desk and lifted, surprised at how heavy it was. Tucked between those luscious curves of hers was solid muscle. "I appreciate your concern, but as I told you earlier, it's not necessary."

Satisfied that the desk was in a safe place, she turned toward the fireplace, her hands on her hips. "A fire's not a good idea. Smoke can give away your whereabouts."

"So can a frozen corpse," he muttered.

She picked up her duffel bag and flung it over her shoulder.

"You forgot something," he said, picking her survival kit off the floor.

She regarded him with cool appraising eyes before taking the tin box from him.

He stared at the back of her tanned legs as she climbed the stairs. He couldn't seem to help himself. "How do you like your steak?"

She dropped her duffel bag on the second floor landing. "Medium."

He nodded in approval. "My specialty. Dinner will be ready in an hour. In the meantime, make yourself comfortable."

He spotted a condom on the floor, picked up the foil packet and shoved it into his pocket. It looked like the lady bodyguard had come prepared for a whole school of sharks.

4

"THE MAN'S GOTTA BE kidding!" Jacquie muttered to herself. First he discredits her, then he fires her. Then he tells her to make herself comfortable. "Yeah, right."

She tossed her survival kit onto the neatly made bed and glanced around. It was a small room with a single window facing the lake, and a ceiling so low that in places she had to duck to keep from bumping her head. But it would do, and it was infinitely better than trying to find her way down the mountain after dark.

She flung her duffel bag into a corner. To think she'd traveled all this way for nothing. Maybe it was just as well. If Rick Westley was that opposed to having a woman bodyguard, then she wanted no part of the job. She'd have to find another way to prove herself to her aunt.

It was his loss. If what Mark had told her was true, Mr. Rick Westley needed her a heck of a lot more than she needed him. If a mad bomber really was out to get him, Rick's dreamy blue eyes would certainly not save him, nor would his devastating smile. Only a professional like herself could protect him.

The problem was, after the fiasco with her survival kit, the chances of him taking her seriously were pretty remote, no matter what she did. She shuddered to think what must be going through his mind. No doubt he thought she was a flake. And it was all her father's fault.

Her father insisted—absolutely *insisted*—that each of his four children carry a survival kit like the one that had saved his life during the Vietnam War. He wasn't much of a protector, her father, not in the family sense, but he meant well.

Regarded as one of the best defense lawyers in the country, he had rescued a number of people facing death row, some of them actually innocent. But like many men brilliant in their fields, he was completely inept in his private life, and even something as mundane as meeting with a teacher to discuss one of his children's behavior problems had turned the otherwise self-confident and brazen criminal lawyer into a bumbling, insecure man.

Maybe that's why Jacquie couldn't bring herself to abandon the habit of carrying the survival kit, even now. It was the one tangible way she could tell herself he really cared about her welfare.

Not that she expected to come face-to-face with sharks. At the rate she was going, she'd be lucky to land a job protecting a sand pile in the Mojave Desert.

Well, despite what Rick Westley might think of her, he had himself a first-rate bodyguard, at least until morning. She had no intention of having yet another client failure on her conscience.

After rummaging through her bag, she changed out of her shorts into a pair of blue jeans and exchanged her sandals for sturdy hiking boots. She patted the slight bulge beneath her vest.

Not all bodyguards were armed, of course, and her aunt left the decision to carry a weapon up to each individual agent. But Jacquie figured she owed it to her clients to provide them with as much protection as possible. Let anyone threaten one of her clients, and she wouldn't hesitate to fire.

Downstairs, the cheerful sound of pots and pans greeted her. "I'm going to check outside," she called.

Westley stepped into the living room wearing an apron, and her heart practically did a tap dance. Had she known an apron could look that sexy, she might have given culinary school one more chance.

"Don't bother," he said. "I mean, I fired you, remember? Why don't you just relax?"

"You said you were paying me for tonight."

"And I fully intend to."

"Then that entitles you to protection." Her eyes locked with his. Just let him laugh, and so help her, she really *would* flip him to the floor.

Lucky for him, he didn't laugh. Lucky for *her*, he didn't even crack one of those sexy smiles of his.

"Someone tried to kill you once, and I mean to see that he or she doesn't succeed the next time. At least not while I'm on the premises. Watch that window."

To emphasize she meant business, she pulled the small-frame .45 automatic out of her shoulder holster, checked it, then slipped it back beneath her vest.

By the look on his face, he obviously didn't know a thing about guns, but she was willing to bet he knew intimidating power when he saw it.

With his gaze still on the slight bulge beneath her vest, he looked more dubious than ever. "I told you, I'm not certain my life really *is* in danger."

The man was obviously in denial. "I'd say a bomb is a pretty good sign you're on somebody's hit list."

She reached into one of the boxes and grabbed a pair of binoculars, an inspection mirror and a small flashlight. She needed the mirror and flashlight to check the car for bombs or signs of tampering.

That red Blazer was begging for a bomb, parked the way it was out in the open. What she would give for an honest-to-goodness garage. Actually, she'd settle for something as simple as a dead bolt on the front door of the cabin, instead of that flimsy lock.

"Don't open the door until I get back. And for Pete's sake, stay out of the killing zone." She indicated the area in front of the large picture window. With a brusque nod, she opened the door a crack and peered outside. After she was satisfied that the coast was clear, she left the cabin, locking the door behind her.

Rick sauntered back into the kitchen, rubbing his temple. *The killing zone?* Were all bodyguards that paranoid or was he just lucky?

He didn't know how effective Jack would be if she actually came face-to-face with a real threat. He hoped never to find out. He suspected that no matter what the danger to herself, she would fight to the bitter end to save him. She was that kind of woman.

And that was the unnerving part. With a woman like her around, he was having the worst time keeping his mind on his work. Normally, work was all he thought about, even during his few off-hours.

His boss might have sent him to the cabin for safety, but Rick's reason for agreeing to come was the peaceful work environment it offered. He was not here to keep track of his bodyguard.

Still, he couldn't resist taking a long hard look out the kitchen window. His body tensed as she came into sight, walking toward the lake. A late afternoon breeze fluffed her hair, and the amber rays of the sinking sun turned the feathery strands into fiery red flames.

Moving with the feral grace of a mountain lion, her body had a language all its own—and every sexy message spoke to his lonely heart.

Startled, he straightened. He didn't have a *lonely* heart. He was happy with his life. A confirmed bachelor, he could come and go as he pleased, work all night if he wanted to and never have to worry about living up to a woman's expectations. That's how he liked it.

Just because he couldn't keep his eyes off this particular woman didn't mean a thing. It certainly didn't mean he had any intention of giving up his cherished life-style.

That settled firmly in his mind, he leaned forward to get a better look at her.

All too soon, she was swallowed up by the woods. He craned his neck, trying to catch another glimpse of her, but to no avail. Irritated at his uncharacteristic fascination with his guest, he turned away from the window, frowning. *The killing zone, indeed!*

JACQUIE STOOD BY THE LAKE peering through her binoculars at the opposite shore. As far as she could tell, this was the only cabin for miles around.

Turning, she swung the binoculars in the direction of Rick's cabin. Pulling the glasses away from her face, she continued to stare at the cabin, her eyes narrowed against the glare of the late afternoon sun shining off the windows. The area looked as peaceful as a picture-perfect postcard.

The cabin blended in with its surroundings, and that was a plus. The place could be easily missed, especially if the windows were blacked out at night to keep the light from showing.

On the other hand, Rick, with his handsome looks and driving energy, probably stood out anywhere, even in a crowd. The last thing a bodyguard wanted was a client that noticeable. Celebrities were the bane of the profession. Rick was no celebrity, but she'd hate to have to guard him in public. Especially around women.

Feeling her heart flutter, she silently repeated, *Thou shalt not lust after clients.*

She turned away from the cabin with a sigh. *So who's lusting?* She was simply doing her job, and part of that job was getting to know her client. That included knowing his strengths and his flaws. It was important for her to know what to expect from him during a crisis or other emergency situation.

Okay, so he was her client only until morning, and the chances of something happening that night were probably zilch. She would at least have the satisfaction of knowing she'd given him the best possible protection during the short time he was under her care. It wasn't much, but it was the best she could do.

She wandered along the curving shoreline and leaped over a marshy area. One foot landing in the water, she moved to dry ground before stopping to scrape the mud off her boot with a stick. She then continued on her way.

The lake shimmered in the late afternoon sun, still as glass. A duck drifted across the serene water, leaving ripples in its wake. Farther out, a silvery trout jumped up, then hit the water with a splash.

She followed a path through a grove of quaking aspens, momentarily losing sight of the lake. A short distance ahead, the trees parted, giving her a full view of a small wooden dock.

A movement there, near a rowboat tied to the pier, made her stop in her tracks. She spotted a man wearing a black leather jacket and a black cap, and called to him. "Hello, there."

The man looked up briefly, then ran. Pulling out her gun, she chased after him, but he disappeared before she reached the dock. Replacing her weapon, she went on to check the rowboat. The bottom of the boat was dry and covered with dead pine needles; obviously, it hadn't been used in quite some time.

The stranger was probably a poacher or someone fishing without a license. Suddenly, the quiet was broken by the sound of a motorcycle. Jacquie waited until the sound had faded away before heading back to the cabin.

She trudged back to where Westley's vehicle was parked. A thorough search for bombs would take a full two hours. Since it would soon be dark, she had time for only a preliminary check.

One of a bodyguard's first tasks was to get to know a client's car inside and out. *Thou shalt inspect a client's car as if it were a lover's body.* You didn't forget rules like that.

She scanned the red paint, looking for any fingerprints or grease marks that might indicate someone had recently tampered with it. A thin layer of road dust covered the body, but otherwise it looked untouched.

She pulled her flashlight out of her pack and scooted under the car. She looked for anything out of the ordinary—fresh paint, bright metal, dirty areas or extra wires. She positioned the inspection mirror and checked on top of the fuel tank, a favorite hiding place for bombers. Nothing. Satisfied that the bottom of the car was clean, she stood, brushing herself off.

She needed to inspect under the hood and inside of the car, but the doors were locked. She pulled a can of talcum powder out of her pack and sprinkled a light coating around the vehicle. No man or beast could come anywhere near that car during the night without her knowing about it in the morning.

After another quick glance around, she knocked on the cabin door. "It's me. Jack. Open up."

5

RICK DIDN'T SEEM particularly concerned that a stranger had been seen hanging around the little dock. "Falcon Heights is a resort town. The area's full of people. No doubt it was a fisherman who thought he'd found a new spot."

Rick was probably right, but Jacquie didn't intend to take any chances. While he tended their steaks, she checked the locks on all the windows, both upstairs and down.

"I hope you like red wine," he called to her from the bottom of the stairs.

"I don't drink when I'm working," she called back. The windows securely locked, she pulled out her cellular phone and punched in the number of the office. It wasn't yet six. Mark, or even Charilyn, her aunt's office manager, should still be there.

Unfortunately, Jacquie was out of range. Sighing, she tucked her phone back into her canvas bag. Satisfied that she'd done as much as she could do for now, she followed the savory smells to the kitchen.

Her host was bent over the sink. With his back toward her, he was less distracting, though heaven knew, not *much* less. For one thing, he had the sexiest tush....

"So what does a bodyguard do, exactly?" He turned unexpectedly and caught her red-handed. "Besides watch a client's ass?"

She lifted her eyes to meet his gaze. Damn, how was she going to bluff her way out of this one? "It's my job to check security," she said, blushing.

"Security, huh?" Rick dried his hands and uncorked a bottle of red wine. "Is that inside or outside the killing zone?"

She glared at him. "You might think it's a joke, but I take my job very seriously. Now if you don't mind, I need to use your phone."

"Sorry, I don't have one."

"No phone?" She glanced around in disbelief. Who ever heard of such a thing?

"The cabin hasn't been used in over a year," he explained. "Besides, I came here to work, not to socialize."

"I was told you were sent here as a safety precaution."

"That, too."

"I've seen doghouses with better security."

Glancing out the kitchen window, she rose to her tiptoes and pulled down the window shade.

"Dinner is served, *Mademoiselle*," he said, feigning a French accent. He pulled out a chair and gave it a quick brush with a dish towel before inviting her, with a sweeping motion of his arm, to sit.

"I think I better sit over here," she said, choosing the chair that provided a full view of the living room and front door.

He pointed to a chair opposite her. "Would it be okay if I sit here, or is this in the killing zone, too?"

She was tempted to respond to his teasing tone in kind, but she wasn't about to make light of anything involving his safety. "That chair's fine," she said, because it was.

Dinner was delicious. Rick was a terrific cook, though she doubted he much enjoyed his meal. He was too busy staring at the monitor of his laptop. Not that she was complaining. His occupied mind gave her ample opportunity to study him without being detected.

Thou shalt know thy client like a lover's body. Startled by the thought, she took a quick sip of water to keep from choking on a piece of meat. Rick glanced up and she gave him a weak smile to indicate she was okay.

He went back to work and she sat rigidly in her chair, unable to move. She'd mixed up the wording of the commandments. She was supposed to check a client's car like a lover's body, not the client.

Thou shalt know thy client. Period! That's what it was. Or was it? Maybe there was something about a lover's body in there somewhere. However it was worded, she owed it to her aunt to fulfill the requirements of the job to the best of her ability.

Settling back so she could best enjoy—uh, study Rick, she noted every nuance that crossed his handsome face. At times, he looked almost at odds with his computer, the world or maybe both. His frown increased even as his fingers raced ever faster over the keyboard.

For an uneasy moment, he reminded her of her father, who never could just sit and relax. Work, work, work, that's all her father ever did. He'd even brought work to the hospital while her mother lay on her deathbed.

A cloud of depression settled over Jacquie and she pushed the memories aside. The last thing she needed in her life was a man like Rick Westley. Thank God she had the good sense to know it.

She finished her dinner and thought about facing Aunt Samantha. How was Jacquie going to explain yet another failure? Maybe it was just as well her cell phone didn't work. She was in no particular hurry to break the news that she had been fired within minutes of reporting to her job. Three months as a bodyguard and she had yet to prove herself.

All her life Jacquie had lived in an overachieving family. Nothing she ever did could possibly compare to the international acclaim of her mother's writing, or her father's tactics in the courtroom. And it wasn't only her parents whose footsteps were too big to fill. Two of her three younger brothers had already made a name for themselves in their respective fields. Her youngest brother, Teddy, had recently graduated from high school with honors.

She was proud of her family, but just once—*once*—she wanted to appear successful in their eyes.

"I plan to leave first thing in the morning," she said, hoping that Rick would change his mind and tell her to stay.

He looked up, a frown cutting into his features. "Do you want me to make the check out to you or the, uh…?"

She tried not to let her disappointment show. "Make the check out to the S. J. Spade Insurance Agency."

He nodded and went back to his laptop.

She leaned to the side so she could see the monitor of his computer. "It must be something pretty important you're working on."

"Just a software program," he replied. "Know anything about computers?"

"I know how to send E-mail and surf the net. Just don't ask me to explain how the things work."

He studied her intently, all-business. "I'm designing a program that will permit software programs to communicate."

"I take it that's a good thing," she said.

"It'll be a boon for consumers."

"It doesn't sound like something worth killing for."

His dimple deepened and she almost forgot to breathe. "Trust me, it's not."

"So why do you suppose somebody sent you a bomb?"

"I have no idea."

"Any enemies?"

"None."

"How can you be so sure?"

He gazed into her eyes. "I'm a lovable guy."

She frowned in irritation. Normally she liked a man with a sense of humor, but being threatened by a mail bomb was no laughing matter. "Any disgruntled employees?'' she persisted. She leveled her gaze at him. ''Maybe someone you fired?''

His face grew serious. ''Believe it or not, you are the first person I ever fired.''

''Really? You did a commendable job. Of all the times I've been let go, I would say yours was the least painful.''

He rubbed his upper lip. ''You've been fired before, have you?''

''Altogether, I've been fired three times.'' She held up the appropriate number of fingers. ''The first time was when I was only eleven. I was fired from my paper route for throwing a newspaper onto a roof and shorting out the Christmas lights. It was a miracle the whole house didn't burn down.''

''And the second time?'' he asked, his eyes lit with avid curiosity.

''The second time was in high school. I worked in a dress shop and was fired for talking a prospective customer out of a designer suit. I couldn't help myself. The suit made the woman look like a blimp. The customer appreciated my honesty. The manager chased me out of the store with a broom.''

''I'm sorry,'' Rick drawled. ''I was kind of hoping I was your first.''

Even had she missed the deep sensual undertone of his voice, the soft flare of interest in his eyes had nothing to do with his work. If the air that sizzled between them was any indication, they were both in serious danger of breaking each and every one of her aunt's commandments about not mixing business with pleasure.

Thinking quickly, Jacquie blurted out the first thing that came to mind. "Any ex-wives, ex-girlfriends, jealous lovers?"

The question seemed to throw him. "What?"

"You'd be amazed at how many jilted lovers retaliate by sending bombs and other dangerous objects in the mail. A woman in Arizona actually sent her ex-lover a live rattlesnake."

He grimaced. "Ow!"

"Then there was the woman who cut off her husband's—"

Shuddering, he held up his hands as if to hold back a falling wall. "Yes, I recall the news reports," he groaned. "I assure you the women in my past have only fond memories of me."

Jacquie sat back in her chair and considered the look of satisfaction on his face. He must harbor a few fond memories of his own, and for some odd reason, this irritated her. "Of course, there's always the possibility you've overestimated your appeal."

His eyes shone with mischief. Obviously, he enjoyed egging her on. "Not a chance."

"Then we have to believe that someone tried to kill you for no reason whatsoever."

"There you go again. Sounding like an FBI agent."

She dabbed at her mouth with a paper napkin. "I'm just trying to get a handle on the facts. One of my jobs as bodyguard is to make out a threat-assessment file on everyone you know. Friends, family, co-workers."

"I hate to disappoint you, but as I've already told you, I have no enemies. What about you? Any ex-husbands or former lovers?"

"None that you'll ever know about." The tone she used was meant to discourage any more questions.

"You can ask me personal questions, but I can't ask them of you. Is that how it works?"

"No one is trying to kill *me*," she said pointedly.

"And I'm not convinced anyone *is* out to kill me. The bomb was some crackpot's idea of a joke."

"If you really believe that, why are you hiding out here in the middle of nowhere?"

"Believe me, this wasn't my idea."

"I see." She finished her meal in silence. Her job was to keep him safe, not conduct an investigation. Still, she couldn't help herself. Her mind reeled with curiosity. Who would want to see him dead and why?

If it wasn't an ex-lover or business acquaintance, then who? While she occupied herself thinking up possible motives, Rick worked on his computer, leaving half his steak and the entire baked potato on his plate, untouched.

Despite Rick's reassurances, she couldn't shake the uneasy feeling that there was more to this bomb business than met the eye.

Rick Westley might be a drop-dead gorgeous computer whiz, but he didn't know beans about crackpots. And what he didn't know could be the death of him.

6

AFTER DINNER, Rick insisted upon cleaning up the kitchen himself. Not that he had a burning desire to wash dishes. Had he been alone, he would have left them to soak, or avoided them altogether by using paper plates. But he needed to clear his mind, and since his bodyguard refused to let him take a walk, scrubbing pots and pans offered a way to work out his frustrations.

His *bodyguard?* He couldn't believe it. What the hell was he doing with a bodyguard?

She was a major distraction. She'd drilled him all through dinner, or at least part of it. But even during the short time she'd sat quietly, he was aware of her presence, aware that she was watching his every move—and it was damn unnerving.

No matter how much he tried to focus on his laptop, no matter how much he pretended she wasn't in the room, he was aware of her, drawn to her.

Who would ever believe he was having trouble concentrating on work, for Pete's sake? Not Mary Allison, who'd moved out of his apartment two years ago and was gone for three days before he actually got around to noticing.

Not his co-workers, who couldn't even persuade him to stop working long enough to attend last year's Christmas party. Not his widowed mother, whom he'd not seen in three years, though he managed to call her every week without fail. Hell, even *he* was having trouble believing he could be so distracted.

Rick leaned back, craning his neck. Now he had a clear view of the living room, but it was Jack he was looking at, nothing else.

She sat on the couch, her legs tucked beneath her. She was filling out those confounded forms of hers, but judging by the faraway look on her face, she could just as easily be composing a love letter or writing in her diary.

Her face had a warm golden glow that was partly due to the reflection of the fire, but mainly seemed to come from some inner source. It surprised him how soft and feminine, even vulnerable, she looked, especially now that she had dropped the tough-guy stance of hers. And her lips…oh, hell, she looked good enough to kiss!

And that's exactly what he wanted to do. Take her in his arms and kiss her. Hold her. Protect her. That and a whole lot more. Small as she was, and as fiery, he'd bet she packed quite a wallop between the sheets.

The last thought jolted him in more ways than one. It had been a long time since a woman had affected him quite like this. He pulled himself forward and stared into the soapy dishwater.

It was crazy. The woman didn't need protecting and he sure as hell didn't need any romantic entanglements.

Irritated to find himself distracted by her, even

when she wasn't in the room, he stared at the dinner plate he'd been scrubbing for several minutes.

Heaving a sigh, he dipped the plate into the rinse water and stacked it in the drying rack.

Work, that's what he should be thinking about. Work. So why wasn't he? Was it the strange surroundings? The fresh air? The altitude? Hell, for all he knew, the volcano that had been causing all the geological unrest in Falcon Heights in recent years was sending out electrical impulses affecting his brain.

Or maybe the damn woman was trying to distract him on purpose. Perhaps this was some sort of ploy bodyguards used to gain control over their clients. Well, no more. From now on, he would simply ignore her.

He planned to work for an hour or two that night, then turn in. After a good night's sleep, he would get an early start in the morning. With a little luck, he might even make up for all the time he'd lost today. Once Jack had gone on her way, nothing, but nothing would distract him from his work!

JACQUIE HATED PAPERWORK, but there was no getting out of it. Her aunt required employees to fill out a full report, citing any security problems on the property and surrounding area.

Jacquie hardly knew where to start. She sat cross-legged on the couch, her bare feet tucked beneath her, and chewed on her pen. She debated what to write on the blank line next to the client's name. *Sexy, handsome, arrogant* were all words that came to mind.

She leaned back and glanced into the kitchen. Rick was still washing dishes. Judging by the meticulous way he scrubbed each plate, he was a perfectionist. She was tempted to fill in the blank with the word *workhorse*. She finally settled on *uncooperative*.

She then listed each of the numerous security problems she'd encountered, starting with the narrow, seventeen-mile dirt road leading to the cabin.

Normally, she would be required to complete a protectee personnel file, but since she was leaving in the morning, she left most of the spaces blank.

She was still pondering over the paperwork when Rick walked into the living room. Ignoring her, he set his laptop on his desk, then sat down with his back to her and immediately began work.

She returned to her report, but she could hardly keep her eyes open. Yawning, she finally stood. It was still early, but the long drive and cool mountain air had sapped her energy. "I'll probably be gone by the time you get up tomorrow," she said.

He looked up from his laptop. "I'm sorry you came all the way out here for nothing."

"I hope for your sake it *was* for nothing." After a moment, she added, "Good night." She hesitated, but only because he was looking at her in such a way that she could hardly breathe. The flames of the dying fire danced in his eyes and her heart beat faster in response. "F-for your own p-peace of mind, I think you should change the lock on the door," she stammered.

"It won't be easy to get someone to come all the way out here just to change a lock."

"Maybe…" She cleared her throat. "Maybe you could add one of those safety chains."

"I suppose I could do that. Jack…earlier, I didn't mean to imply…I'm sure you're a very competent bodyguard."

For no good reason, she blushed. "No—no problem." She turned and climbed the stairs without a backward glance. But the heat of his gaze boring into her shoulder blades was a tangible force that propelled her quickly to the safety of the loft.

She finally understood why so many of her aunt's on-the-job commandments had to do with client-employee relationships.

The nature of the job forced an intimacy not found in the usual workplace. Jacquie hadn't fought off this many temptations since the day she was separated from her Girl Scout troop and accidentally got locked inside a chocolate factory. At the age of ten, she'd nearly starved to death rather than steal so much as a bite of candy. But that was then. Now, she wasn't quite so noble.

Sighing, she reached into her bag for her night attire. Not that she was *that* interested in Rick Westley, of course. Oh, sure, he was handsome and sexy and had a body to die for. Physically, he made her feminine pulses race. Intellectually, he definitely was not her type.

Stripping, she donned an oversize Garfield T-shirt and slid her gun underneath the bed where she could reach it quickly, if necessary.

The window in her room was louvered, making it impossible for anyone to enter, so she left it open a tiny crack. She climbed beneath the covers as the sound of croaking frogs drifted into her room, along with the sweet fragrance of fir trees.

The pine-scented air reminded her of her office. How she dreaded the thought of facing her aunt. Rick Westley could say what he wanted, but the real reason he hadn't wanted her to stay was because she was a woman.

It was the second time in so many days that she had been fired because of her sex.

After the great poodle fiasco, her aunt had assigned her to accompany a jeweler to New York. The man had taken one look at Jacquie and demanded another bodyguard. Her aunt refused to give in to the store owner's demands, and her agency had lost the account. Needless to say, Jacquie felt terrible. It seemed she'd caused her aunt nothing but trouble since starting work. And now this.

Jacquie turned over and pounded her pillow with her fist. Ohhh, it made her so mad. She'd always wanted to be a policewoman, but when she failed the physical requirements because of her small stature, she'd gone to business school.

It didn't take long to figure out she was more suited to law enforcement than the corporate world, and so at her father's insistence, she'd entered law school.

She'd thought this would please him, but not so.

Not until she agreed to stay away from the criminal element and pursue corporate law did he even acknowledge she was a law student, but still he offered little support. If he had, she might have stuck it out and stayed in school, no matter how much she hated it.

What she really wanted to do was be a private investigator. It's what she'd always wanted, though it had taken her a long time to figure it out.

She'd been so blinded by the need to please her family that she had ignored the obvious: solving crimes, maintaining law and order were in her blood. Why couldn't her father accept this about her? Though he was a criminal lawyer, he maintained that it was no job for a woman.

Her father had never quite gotten over Jacquie's mother being a mystery writer. He might have forgiven her had she written cozy English mysteries, where violence was considered bad form, and poison the only civilized way to commit murder. Instead, her mother had written gritty stories about serial killers.

For years, he'd showered her mother with romance novels, obviously thinking romance was a more suitable genre for a woman writer. But her mother could be as stubborn as her sister, Samantha, when she wanted to be. She'd written her gritty, slasher-type stories almost to the day she died.

Jacquie felt a heaviness in her heart as painful memories assailed her—of the way her mother used to throw out plot ideas for the family to mull over. Jacquie had grown up thinking it was normal for families to sit around the dinner table plotting murders. How she missed her mother!

It took a while, but the memories finally faded away and she drifted toward sleep reciting her aunt's commandment: *Thou shalt not lust after your client.*

Jacquie's eyes flew open. So who was lusting? She punched her pillow again and turned over.

She woke later that night with a start and lay perfectly still, trying to figure out what had wakened her. At first she thought it was Lord Byron. The damn dog had probably succumbed to another lust attack and escaped again.

Then she remembered the poodle had probably been sent to the great fire hydrant in the sky, for all she knew, and she was alone in the bed—just as Rick was alone in *his* bed.

She didn't have time to dwell on this sorry state of affairs when something—a rattling sound— came drifting through the darkness.

She lifted her head off the pillow and strained her ears. At first she thought it might be the wind, but then a soft shuffle came from the direction of the stairs, followed by a muffled thud.

Alarmed, she jumped out of bed and reached for her gun. Someone was trying to break into the cabin.

With no time to lose, she crept silently across the room, the smooth wooden floor cool beneath her bare feet, and peered down the staircase.

A ribbon of satiny moonlight streamed through the window in the front room, but otherwise the cabin was dark.

She stood at the top of the stairs, her head cocked. All was quiet. Slowly she descended the stairs, halting momentarily when a wooden step creaked beneath her feet.

Upon reaching the first floor, she heard another sound, this time coming from the kitchen. She was willing to bet the intruder was the same man she had spotted by the boat dock before dinner.

Her back against the wall, she waited for him to enter the front room.

Suddenly, a hand clamped down on her wrist, startling her. Reacting instinctively, she sliced the air with a quick chop, hitting the man's arm with the side of her hand.

She brought up her knee, catching him where it counted. He groaned in pain and let go of her wrist. Before he had a chance to recover, she yanked back on his hand and flipped him head over heels to the floor.

Jamming the barrel of her gun to his head, she ran her free hand along the wall. "Don't move, mister."

She flicked on the wall switch and blinked against the bright light that flooded the room. Staring at the form sprawled on the floor, she blinked again, not wanting to believe the scene in front of her. "Mr. Westley!" she gasped.

Her client lay at her feet, naked except for the skimpiest, not to mention sexiest, pair of briefs she'd ever seen on a man—except, perhaps, in a plain-wrap mail-order catalogue. "What are you doing here?"

Looking as if he was having difficulty focusing,

he rubbed the back of his head and emitted a low, pitiful groan. "I believe you put me here."

Falling to her knees by his side, she laid her gun on the floor. "Mr. Westley...Rick...where does it hurt?" From the way he was groaning, she feared nothing short of major surgery could repair the damage. His head rolled back and his eyes fluttered shut.

"Come on, Westley, stay with me." She gently slapped his cheeks, then frantically ran her hands up and down his near naked body, checking for injuries. "Come on, now. Talk to me. I lost Lord Byron. Please don't let me lose another client."

He opened one eye. "You lost a lord?" His voice sounded strained, as if it cost him to utter even a single syllable.

She pulled back and eyed him with suspicion. "I thought you were injured."

"I am," he said, emitting another groan. "I'm in agony."

Her first impulse was to run for the phone; then she remembered the cabin didn't have one and hers was out of range. So much for modern technology. "Tell me where you hurt?"

"My head, my leg, my..." His voice faded away.

Gingerly, she touched her fingers to his thigh. "Not bad," she said. "I mean..." She chanced a quick glance at him. "I can't see where you're hurt."

"Higher." He sounded weaker.

She quickly moved her fingers upward. His muscles tensed beneath her touch, but whether from pain or something else was hard to say. A sensuous glance passed between them, and feeling as if she'd suddenly been burned, she pulled her hand away.

"My back," he whispered, his face white.

Chiding herself for her suspicious nature, she followed his instructions. The man wasn't joking; he *was* in pain, and it was up to her to do something about it.

Finding no bumps or bruises on his thighs or back, she turned her attention to the rest of his magnificent, uh, prone body.

Drawing from her extensive training, she used her powers of observation to full advantage. When she wrote up the accident report that her aunt's insurance company required, she wanted to be accurate. Pride in her work demanded it. Her aunt demanded it.

Her hands traveled down the length of him and she did a mental checklist. Taut stomach. Broad shoulders. Strong pecs. Tight buns. Nice aftershave...

His muscular chest was covered with a light sprinkling of crisp golden hairs that matched those on his arms and legs. Not a single bruise or bump marked his body, as far as she could tell, but she ran her hands over him again—taking her own sweet time—just to make certain. No one would ever accuse her of leaving a stone unturned—or a pec unchecked.

Satisfied that there was nothing too wrong with him, she inadvertently rested a hand on the hard ridge that rose beneath his Jockey shorts.

He jumped and she screamed. She couldn't believe it; she actually screamed.

Her cheeks flaring, she covered her mouth and stared at him from over her fingertips.

He grimaced as he reached for the small of his back. "Now you've done it," he complained, his voice husky. "My back really *is* out."

"Oh, dear!" She jumped to her feet. "Don't move. I'll only be a sec." She then did what any well-trained professional would do under the circumstances: she raced upstairs to retrieve her box of condoms.

7

RICK WAS STILL SPRAWLED on the floor when Jacquie returned moments later with her survival kit. Dropping to her knees by his side, she dumped out the contents of the metal case, and frantically searched through the supplies. "Where is it?" she muttered. There had to be something here for back injuries.

Rick's moans sounded like a cross between a charging bear and someone about to give birth. She leaned over him. "Mr. Westley? Are you able to get up?"

He stared at the condoms scattered on the floor and shook his head, looking about as miserable as a man could look. "Don't I wish!"

"What?"

"Never mind. Ow!"

Alarmed, she trailed her fingers over his forehead. "I'm taking you to Emergency," she said.

An iron grip circled her wrist. "I don't need to go to the hospital," he whispered. "I need..."

His voice faded away and she leaned closer. "Tell me, what do you need?"

"I need..." He surprised her by folding an arm around her middle and closing the gap between them. Though her breasts were pressed against his bare chest, she decided not to mention her aunt's commandment forbidding compromising positions. The poor man had no idea what he was doing.

"Tell me what—" He cupped her face in his hands and coaxed her head closer, until their noses practically touched. She inhaled softly. "Mr.—" The rest of her sentence was lost the instant his hot demanding lips covered her mouth.

Shocked by this sudden turn of events, she tried to think of a tactful way to resist his advances. The poor man was obviously in shock—or better be!

While she tried to decide what to do, she kissed him back; it seemed only right under the circumstances. Wasn't that what she had learned in bodyguard boot camp? To keep an injured party flat on his back and his mind off his pain?

While she was busy applying this special brand of first aid, he proceeded to devour her with hungry kisses until her whirling senses exploded into sizzling flames.

In the fuzzy recesses of her brain, it occurred to her that maybe this wasn't the right brand of medicine. She wondered if perhaps she might be making his injuries worse.

Oh, what the heck. Leaning against him, she surrendered completely. It was the only way she could position herself so as to return his kisses unhampered and with equal intensity.

Hmm, nice, she thought, savoring the taste and feel of him, inhaling the manly fragrance of his heated body. *Very nice.*

It wasn't until his hand grazed her breast that

something resembling sanity took hold. *Thou shalt not!*

How she found the strength to pull away, she'd never know. "I don't think—" she gasped.

"Good," he drawled softly. "No one should think at times like this." She opened her mouth to protest, but he crushed her in his arms again and stopped her with a not so gentle thrust of his tongue.

Oh, heavenly days! She relaxed against him, feeling a thrill inside as his tongue did a playful dance in every secret recess of her mouth. *Aunt Samantha will kill me.*

Her hand brushed against the front of his Jockey shorts for the second time that night, but whether it was by accident or intent, she didn't want to know.

She didn't scream, not this time, but reality hit her like a ton of bricks.

Thou shalt not play with fire! It wasn't one of Samantha's commandments, but it should be!

Against her better judgment, Jacquie lingered in his arms, absorbing every wonderful and forbidden sensation until she felt dizzy. She was playing with fire, all right. Warm, tantalizing, delicious and desirable fire, but fire, nonetheless.

He stroked her thigh with gentle fingers, leaving a trail of silky warmth in the wake of his touch. His hand traveled beneath her T-shirt and he followed the line of her panties with one heated fingertip, before tugging at the elastic.

"Mr. Westley!" This time she pushed away from him with all her might. She scrambled to her feet. "You must stay calm!" The fact that she was anything but calm herself was beside the point. "Don't move. It's bad for your back." Not to mention her virtue.

He rested his head on his elbow and gazed up at her, looking as innocent as a babe-in-arms—or at least as innocent as a near naked, aroused man could look. "Sorry, I just wanted to make certain I hadn't sustained any serious injuries. You never know until everything's been tested."

She tugged at the hem of her suddenly inadequate T-shirt, trying to get old Garfield to pay for his keep and stretch to her toes. But the damn fabric cat wasn't cooperating, and the more she tugged at the hem, the lower the neckline drooped.

His heated gaze followed her plunging neckline to her newly exposed cleavage. The look of appreciation in his eyes raised her already hot blood to the boiling point. She quickly released the hem.

"I'm a…" She cleared her voice and started again. "I'm a—a professional bodyguard," she stammered, her voice two octaves higher than normal. "I do not consort with clients."

He sat up slowly, his hand on the small of his back. "I'm not a client. I fired you, remember?"

"That's no reason to sexually harass me!"

"Sexually ha—" His eyes widened in astonishment. "You're the one who flung me to the floor and tried to have your way with me."

"I was *not* trying to have my way with you. I was trying to save your life. I thought you were an intruder!"

He reached for one of the foil-wrapped condoms and studied it. "Lucky for you I'm not. Attack the average intruder with a box of condoms and he's likely to jump to some rather startling conclusions."

She snatched the condom away from him and threw it into the metal box. "Since it's obvious you've fully recovered from your injuries, I'm going back to bed." Packing her emergency kit, she spun around and headed for the stairs, taking them two at a time.

Rick Westley was the most egotistical, most annoying, most...! Plopping herself on the edge of her bed, she tried to think of an appropriate word to describe him. The problem was, her mouth still burned with the heat of his kiss, and that made thinking pretty much out of the question. It was far easier to dwell on the glorious sensation of his mouth on hers.

She jumped to her feet, surprised to find herself trembling. She was torn between leaving the cabin right away or waiting until morning.

The nerve of him! Accusing her of taking advantage of *him!* He was the one who'd first kissed *her.* And just because he made her feel more alive than she'd felt in months, maybe years, did not excuse his unseemly behavior.

How dare he taunt her with his sexy hard body and strong warm arms. Who did he think he was, making her do things, think things, feel things that were in complete violation of her aunt's rules of professional behavior? What right did he have?

Feeling weak and shivery, and too confused to

think straight, Jacquie sat down on the edge of the bed and closed her eyes.

If only things were different. If only she wasn't so hung up on not making the same mistake as her mother had made, maybe then...

No, not even then. Nothing would make Jacquie give in to the urge to go back downstairs and insist they finish what Rick had begun. Her aunt depended on her to do a job and she would not let her down. No matter how great the temptation or how weak the spirit.

What happened, or nearly happened, had been a grave mistake—an occupational hazard, nothing more. You put a normal, healthy man and woman in a cabin in the woods with no one around for miles, and it was bound to lead to a little hanky-panky.

Everyone knew that. It was elementary. That's why Aunt Samantha was so adamant that her agents avoid romantic entanglements.

It was human nature, that's what it was, a Mars and Venus thing. It meant nothing.

Oh, sure, he could kiss like no other man she ever knew. And somehow he had managed to waken a passion within her she hadn't known she was capable of feeling. But she would never be so foolish as to let his amazing kisses blind her to the undeniable fact that she and Rick simply did not share the same values.

Feeling somewhat relieved at having regained control of the situation, she lay stiff as a board on the bed, arms at her sides, and stared at the ceiling.

Yes, indeed, she was in full control, and it was

only a matter of time before her lips would stop burning and the aching need inside fade away.

She was still staring at the ceiling when the first sliver of daylight crept into the room. Not only was she staring, but the memory of his lips continued to blaze, filling her mind with all sorts of amazing possibilities. It wasn't a good sign.

Whatever was going on was bigger than she was. The only solution was to leave the cabin before Rick got up.

Convinced it was the only way, she climbed out of bed, grabbed her duffel bag and tiptoed downstairs. After a quick shower, she'd hightail it down the mountain as fast as humanly possible. If time and distance didn't cure the lust she felt for him, nothing would.

She reached the bottom step before she realized she was not alone. Rick was still on the floor where she'd left him, lying on his right side. Fearing the worst, she tiptoed across the room. He didn't move, and in the dim light of daybreak, he looked pale and lifeless.

She gasped softly. *Dear God, don't let it be true.* She'd never forgive herself if she lost another of Aunt Samantha's clients!

She leaned over him and checked his vital signs. His pulse felt steady, and in the dim morning light she could just barely make out his chest rising and falling.

He was breathing, thank God. She almost collapsed with relief. But if he wasn't dead, what was he doing still sprawled on the floor?

She debated what to do. She would never forgive herself if something was seriously wrong. Or if letting him kiss her had made his injuries worse. Her hand on his bare shoulder, she shook him gently. "Mr. Westley?"

His eyes flickered open.

"What are you doing here?" she asked.

He groaned and reached for his lower back. "I couldn't get up last night. My back..."

"Oh, no!" She felt terrible. Awful. To think she'd left him helpless, deserted him. What kind of a heartless person was she? What kind of a bodyguard? "Why didn't you call for help?"

He gazed at her from beneath lowered lids and she quickly averted her eyes. "Would you have come?"

"Of course I would have." Her face felt hot. "Where does it hurt?" Not wanting to add to his injuries, she tentatively placed a hand on his smooth back between his shoulder blades, feeling his muscles tense beneath her palm.

"Lower," he said, nodding as her fingers trailed to the area below his ribs. "That's it."

"All right. I'm taking you to Emergency."

"I don't have time." He moved his leg, but it obviously pained him to do so. He wasn't faking. Not this time, of that she was certain. "I can't afford to lose any more time. I've got work to do. If you could just help me to the desk."

She shook her head in disbelief. "How do you expect to get any work done if you're in pain?"

"Very carefully," he said, grimacing.

"I'm not leaving until I know you're okay. I'm

not about to lose another…" She stopped herself, but not soon enough.

His eyes widened. "You were going to say client, weren't you? Lord what's his name…" He groaned again.

"Do you think you can stand up if I help you?"

"I don't know." He studied her face. "How many clients have you lost?" When she didn't reply, he persisted. "Come on, fess up. How many?"

Judging by his steady gaze, he wasn't going to drop the subject, no matter how much pain he was in.

Finally, she relented. She had nothing to lose but her pride, and she had precious little of that left. "So far? Only one."

"One out of how many clients?" He gave her a hopeful look. "A thousand? Two thousand?"

She slid an arm beneath his back. "See if you can sit up."

"Don't tell me. I'm only client number two." He meant it jokingly, but when she didn't correct him, he groaned aloud. "Oh, no. And you said I had nothing to worry about as long as you were protecting me."

"I seem to recall you saying something about not needing protection."

"Don't remind me." He lifted his head and tried to pull himself into a sitting position.

He looked so miserable she wanted to kick herself for flipping him to the floor. But when he'd grabbed her in the dark, she'd acted out of instinct.

"That's the way," she said. "Now put your arm around me." He wrapped his arm around her midriff and it felt surprisingly strong. Though the air was cool and the fire had died down, the heat of his hand against her waist seemed to burn right through her T-shirt and into her flesh.

A shiver of awareness shot through her, all the way to her painted toes. Whether by design or chance, he was doing it again—making her feel like a quivery mass of pure feminine lust.

Heart pounding, she slowly, gently, helped him to his feet and prayed that he didn't know what he was doing to her. Of course, if her legs collapsed in a rubbery heap as they threatened to do, he'd know exactly how he affected her.

"There," she said, hardly able to find her voice. "That wasn't so bad, now was it?"

"Just don't ask me to dance. Ouch!"

"Lean on me," she said, sensing that he was holding back as if to protect her. "I can take it." *Yeah, right!*

His eyes locked with hers for a moment before he raised his arm. Her body quivered as his hand closed around her shoulder, but it was sheer determination that allowed her to keep her composure.

Muscles taut, she managed to concentrate on holding him upright. All those hours of pumping iron had paid off. Grimacing, she pressed her hip firmly against his and walked him ever so slowly to the couch.

He lowered himself, but his hand brushed against her breast and she felt the tip harden beneath her shirt.

Inhaling softly, she quickly busied herself arranging the toss pillows behind him, pulling back quickly when her breasts accidentally rubbed against him a second time.

"All right, you win," he said, relaxing against the cushions, his right leg extended to its full length. "I'll go to the doctor. But I'm not wearing any body cast."

She glanced at his half-naked body. "Right now, I'd settle for regular clothes." She tried to keep her voice light, but it would have been easier to lift the cabin off its foundation.

He gave her a sheepish grin. "Sorry. Would you mind getting me something to wear?" He shifted his weight. "A shirt and jeans."

She was only too glad to fetch his clothes. A suit of armor, even. One that covered him from head to toe. "Don't move." She walked into his bedroom, pulled a flannel shirt out of the closet and grabbed a pair of jeans off the back of a chair.

"This okay?" she asked, walking back into the living room.

"It'll do."

It was obvious he wasn't able to dress himself. That meant that *she* would have to dress him.

Oh, heavenly days!

Not knowing where to look, she decided to dress him from the top down, keeping her eyes firmly placed on the task at hand. She carefully worked the sleeve of his shirt up one arm. She then pulled the shirt onto the broad expanse of his shoulder, before starting on the other sleeve.

He looked up at her and she felt herself blush

for no good reason. Leaving his shirt unbuttoned, she pulled back and reached for his jeans.

Aunt Samantha prided herself on training her agents to handle every possible situation. Well, Jacquie had news for the owner of the S. J. Spade Insurance Agency. The grueling Spade boot camp failed to cover one important subject: how to dress a gorgeous bod without breaking a single commandment.

Taking a deep breath, she bent over and lifted his right leg. She then worked his foot into the tapered leg of his pants. She avoided his eyes, but she could feel the heat of his gaze on her face as she pulled the denim fabric up his long powerful leg.

"How'd you learn to flip a man like that?" he asked. She didn't miss the admiration in his voice, and it gave her a warm feeling. "Do you have a black belt?"

"No, nothing like that," she said. The graceful, elegant moves that most people associated with the martial arts were meant for sports or exhibition and not for actual defense purposes. Having learned self-defense tactics from her brothers, Jacquie lacked grace and discipline, but she got the job done.

"I mean for a woman your size…it's amazing."

"It's not size that counts," she explained. "It's balance."

"Really? Balance, huh?" Something in his voice made her look up. The humorous lights in his eyes confirmed her suspicions. He was getting some sort of perverse pleasure from watching her struggle to dress him. "I'll remember that."

Getting him into the jeans was a challenge, but mainly because his nearness made her nervous. She kept thinking that any moment he would grab her like he had the previous night and kiss her again.

Firming her mouth, she watched him from beneath the lush fringe of her lowered lashes. Just let him try to kiss her, she thought, silently challenging him to do that very thing.

This time she was prepared to say no—and mean it—or at least sound as if she meant it. She owed it to her aunt to obey company policy. She owed it to herself.

When he made no attempt to pick up where they'd left off, she tried to relax. If only her trembling fingers didn't keep brushing against his heated flesh and her eyes didn't keep straying to his velvet-soft lips, dressing him would be less torturous.

It wasn't easy to work the pants up his legs and over his manly thighs, but keeping her eyes from wandering to forbidden territory was altogether impossible.

Despite her best efforts, her fingers brushed against his crotch, proving that certain parts of the human body continued to function despite pain. It wasn't often that a medical discovery made her pulses skitter, but everything about Rick turned her into a ball of nervous energy.

She was forced for the second or maybe even the third time that morning to remind herself that she was a professional bodyguard. And no professional worth his or her salt would think of buttoning a client's fly.

Leaving Rick to pull his pants up over his hips, she stood.

"I'm going to take a shower," she said. Actually, she planned on taking a very long, very *cold* shower. Her eyes locked with his. "Then I'll take you to Emergency."

8

OUTSIDE, IT WAS a beautiful, crystal-clear day. Sturdy pines stretched toward the cloudless blue sky, and silver glints of sunlight danced upon the upper branches. Two squirrels chased each other through tall grass strung with pearls of morning dew.

Leaving Rick safely inside, Jacquie made a quick check of the area surrounding the cabin. The lake sparkled like blue topaz, the rugged mountains reflecting on its mirrorlike surface. Patches of snow left over from last winter dotted the weathered crevices and topped the uppermost peaks like a carelessly tossed ermine shawl.

Inhaling the pine-scented air, Jacquie walked around the cabin, tucking pieces of thread into the window frames. She then turned her attention to the red Blazer. Red, of all colors. The car stood out like a sore thumb.

Rick had suggested they take his car, since it was a four-wheel drive. It was a good idea, despite her reservations about the color, but she still hadn't checked the interior or under the hood.

The talcum powder she'd sprinkled around the car the evening before had not been disturbed. That was something.

Inspecting the interior was a breeze, mainly because Rick's car was spotlessly clean. Even the trunk and glove compartment were neat, containing a minimum of car manuals and maps.

She paid special attention to the driver's seat, checking over and under it. *Thou shalt know a client's car like a lover's body.*

Momentarily distracted, she caressed the slight indentation in the leather seat formed by the weight of Rick's body. If she didn't know better, she'd swear she could still feel the heat of him radiating from the spot.

Irritated at herself for letting such thoughts interfere with her work, she quickly pulled her hand away. She planted her feet firmly on the ground and slammed the car door shut.

It took longer to check the engine, but as far as she could tell, there were no unexplained wires or other signs of tampering. Even so, she left nothing to chance.

Bombers were becoming ever more sophisticated, and some had managed to fashion plastic explosives of virtually any size or shape. Only the most thorough search could uncover such a bomb. For this reason, she ran her fingers into every possible nook and cranny she could find until she was certain no bomb existed.

Despite the unfortunate color, Rick's utility vehicle had a lot going for it. The tinted windows provided some protection. The four-wheel drive made it easier to maneuver the car over the rutted dirt road leading into town. There was also a powerful engine, allowing for a quick getaway if necessary.

Once she was satisfied the car was clean, she drove the Blazer as close to the cabin as possible. Rick waited for her on the porch, and just the sight of him quickened her pulse.

Frowning, she climbed out of the car. "I told you to stay inside," she said brusquely.

"Oh, that's right. I forgot. The killing zone."

Ignoring his mocking tone, she moved to his side. She slid one arm around his waist and, keeping a watchful eye on the woods directly opposite the cabin, she helped him to the car, then climbed behind the wheel. His presence seemed to absorb the air in the cab, and the best she could do was breathe in ragged gasps. She cracked the window open and buckled up.

The one thing she had yet to do was brief him. Grateful she had something to do to keep her mind occupied, she set to work as soon as she swung onto the dirt road.

"If you hear me shout 'get down,' do it. Don't ask me why, just do what I say." That was better. She was in control again. Her breathing was almost back to normal. More important, her voice was strong, direct and aloof. Had she not chanced a sideways glance in his direction, she might have almost believed her own act.

She moistened her lower lip. What was the matter with her? Other men had kissed her without affecting her entire being. What made Rick's kisses so different?

They were different, all right. Not only could she not stop thinking about what had transpired between them, the taste of him still lingered in her mouth. Not even the foul-tasting mouthwash she'd used that morning had made it go away.

Another kiss like that and she would be in *b-i-g* trouble. That made two of them. For if he so much as tried anything, she'd do whatever was necessary to protect herself. And if that meant he ended up in a body cast, he would have only himself to blame.

It suddenly occurred to her that he had not responded to her instructions. She pressed her fingers into the steering wheel. "Did you hear what I said?"

"Yeah, I heard." He sounded like he was in pain.

She couldn't help but feel sorry for him. The poor man. With his head against the headrest, his eyes closed, he looked about as miserable as a man could look.

She hated to harp on the subject when he was obviously suffering, but it was imperative he understand she meant business.

"If I say 'get down' it means we're under attack, and it'll make my job a lot easier if you cooperate." There. She'd said it. No more kisses. Or at least that's what she meant to say, and if he had half a brain, he'd know it.

"Do you actually think something's going to happen?" He sounded more surprised than worried.

She glanced at him and this time he was openly watching her. "*Nothing* is going to happen."

"Well then?"

She stared at the road as if her life depended on

it. "We have to be ready for anything. Just remember, you may be my boss, but I'm in charge." *And that means you'll never kiss me again, Rick Westley! So help me God!*

He moved his leg slightly, grimacing. "It looks like I don't have much choice, do I?" He laid his hand on her thigh. "About last night…"

She grasped the steering wheel so hard her knuckles turned white. The man was obsessed. Hell, *she* was obsessed. Her breasts rose and fell as she struggled for air. "Forget it. You were out of your head, like you said."

She was driving too fast, given the condition of the road. Unfortunately, she didn't know this until she hit a rut.

Rick grabbed his lower back. "What are you trying to do? Kill me?"

"Sorry," she muttered beneath her breath, letting up on the gas pedal. If it hadn't been for the seat belts, they would probably have hit their heads on the roof of the car. Heaven only knows what would have happened had he not moved his hand.

She slowed down to a near crawl. "I'm sure you wouldn't have kissed me had…you know. Had you not been out of your head."

He regarded her for a moment. "I was referring to the way you flipped me. It was my fault. I shouldn't have tried to sneak up on you like I did."

There was a long brittle silence between them before anything resembling a normal voice returned to her. "It's nice of you not to blame me but..." She steered around a fallen tree trunk.

"I'm not letting you off the hook completely," he said. "Now that you mentioned it, you *did* kiss me back, you know."

She avoided his eyes. The road was particularly rough in this part of the woods, requiring special attention. "I was afraid I'd make your injuries worse by pushing you away."

"Liar," he growled.

"If you weren't hurting so much, I'd show you how good I am at ejecting an unwanted passenger from the car."

"Is that one of those moves that requires balance?"

She narrowed her eyes against the sudden glare of sunlight that slanted through the trees. "Don't push me, Westley."

He fell silent, but that did nothing to alleviate the tension between them. Her nerves were as taut as a rubber band stretched to the limit.

To say she was overly aware of him would be an understatement. If he moved so much as a muscle, she knew it, felt it, and nothing she did could keep her from sliding a glance in his direction every chance she got.

Halfway to town, a deer bounded across the road. Her foot flew to the brake pedal and the car came to a sudden stop.

The deer disappeared into the thick growth, but she was reluctant to drive on. The view was breathtakingly beautiful and she couldn't pull her eyes away. "It's gorgeous!" she whispered.

Falcon Heights had suffered economically in recent years due to the increase in seismic activity. Molten rock moved below the earth's surface, and scientists predicted the long-dormant volcano would erupt for the first time in two hundred and fifty years.

As late as last spring, as many as two thousand earthquakes were recorded in a single week, and officials had called for a condition-yellow watch. But in recent months, there had been no signs of volcanic unrest, and it was hard to imagine that anything could shatter the peaceful serenity of the area.

Rick gazed at the majestic mountains and lush green valley below as if seeing his surroundings for the first time. "It *is* beautiful."

She glanced at him curiously before stepping on the gas. "I'll pay for whatever medical care you need." It would set her back financially, but with the impending lawsuit, it probably wouldn't be wise to file an accident report with her aunt's insurance company. Her aunt would be furious enough as it was without having her insurance rates raised.

"Forget it. I told you I don't blame you. Besides, my insurance will cover my expenses." He rubbed his thigh and she was instantly reminded of the warm flesh and strong muscles beneath his jeans. "Have you been working as a bodyguard for long?"

Grateful for the change of subject, she adjusted the air conditioner. "Three months."

"It seems like an odd profession for a woman,"

he said. "Did you always want to be a body-guard?"

"Actually, I plan to open my own private detective agency next year." Up until that moment, only her aunt knew about her plans.

His gaze traveled down the length of her, but at least he didn't laugh. "I'd never take you for a private eye."

"That's an asset when you work undercover."

"I guess it would be."

"If you're thinking of hiring a private investigator to find out who sent you that bomb, I'll be glad to check things out for you. Free of charge."

He looked surprised. "Isn't that the FBI's job?"

"Lots of people hire a private eye after they've been victimized by a crime. You'd be amazed at the number of crimes solved by a P.I. The police get the credit, the P.I. gets the bucks and everyone's happy."

"The bomb was a fluke. Probably sent to me by mistake. To tell you the truth, I don't even know if it was meant for me. I never looked at the address label. I may not have been the target."

"You really believe that, don't you? About the bomb being a fluke?"

"Yeah, I do. I'm not the kind of guy that gets himself knocked off." He frowned as he stared at the road ahead. "Not usually, anyway."

THE EMERGENCY ROOM was crowded with hikers, campers and other tourists, including a family of seven who'd lost a territorial dispute to a swarm of angry bees.

It was an hour before Rick was finally wheeled into an examination room at the end of the corridor.

Jacquie stood guard outside his room. Rick might really believe that bull about the bomb being a fluke, but she wasn't about to take chances.

He walked out of the examination room some forty minutes later, waving a prescription. He was no longer in a wheelchair, but he was stooped over slightly, his hand on the small of his back.

"No broken ribs," he said. "The doctor said to rest and I'll be as good as new in a day or two." He grinned. "It looks like you're not going to lose another client, after all."

She grinned back. "That's good news. Where do we go to fill your prescription?"

"There's a drugstore across the street." Limping slightly, he started toward the sliding glass doors leading to the parking lot.

"Wait." She hurried past him and glanced outside before motioning to him. "Remember, do exactly what I say." She slid on sunglasses to hide her eyes. It was an old Secret Service trick that allowed security agents to scan the area without being detected.

Letting him walk ahead of her, she followed one pace behind. It was important to keep the eyes moving at all times.

A man stood across the street, leaning against a lamppost. It was hard to know for certain, but it could be the same man she'd spotted at the boat dock by Rick's cabin. Her senses on full alert, she edged closer to Rick.

The man put his hand in his pocket and pulled out something shiny.

Without a moment's hesitation, she pushed Rick out of the line of fire—and into the path of an oncoming car!

The bumper of the car hit Rick, sending him flying over the hood. Jacquie opened her mouth, but nothing came out.

All she could do was watch helplessly as Rick bounced off the car and landed in a bed of ivy.

9

IT TOOK CONSIDERABLY longer for the doctors to examine Rick the second time. He was x-rayed and checked out by an orthopedic specialist before the admitting doctor finally declared Rick lucky, and none the worse for wear.

"You can get dressed now," Dr. Wong said. He stuck his pen into the pocket of his starched white coat and left the room.

Rick sat on the examining table, his bare legs dangling over the side. He had a bruise the size of a grapefruit on his thigh—and a headache to match—but strangely enough, his back no longer hurt. He wouldn't advise it to his worst enemy, but that little run-in with a car had somehow straightened out his back problems. Who would think such a thing possible?

The doctor had said he was lucky. But despite his miraculous recovery, he didn't feel particularly lucky.

Scooting forward, he planted his feet on the cold linoleum floor and reached for his jeans.

Yep, his back was cured, all right. It was just his nerves that were shot.

That woman bodyguard kissed like an angel, but she was definitely out to kill him!

He shoved his battered legs one by one into his

jeans for the third time that day, and reached for his shirt. A knock sounded at the door. Giving his zipper a quick upward yank, he looked around for his sneakers. "Come in!"

It was Jack, looking oddly benign, given the trouble she'd caused him. "Stay where you are," he said. With a bodyguard like her, he didn't need enemies. "Don't come any closer."

"What's the matter with you? Are you contagious?"

"What's the matter with *me*? What's the matter with *you*?" He shoved his foot into a sneaker. "Twice. You tried to kill me twice."

"I was not trying to kill you," she said. "I was trying to protect you."

"Protect me? First you throw me on the floor, then you throw me in front of a moving car. What kind of protection is that? If it's all the same to you, I think I'll take my chances alone."

"But he had a gun."

He looked up. "Who had a gun?"

"The man across the street. It was the same man I saw at the lake. Rick, please, if you don't want me as your bodyguard, then let me call my aunt and have her assign you another one."

She sounded so worried, he was almost inclined to believe she'd actually seen a man with a gun. "You really believe this guy is out to get me?"

"Yeah, I do."

"But what would be his motive?"

"Contrary to popular belief, not every killer needs a motive."

"Listen, I'm just an ordinary guy who lives an

ordinary, maybe even boring life. I have no ex-wives and I'm still friends with my ex-girlfriends. Until I met you, I lived a peaceful, nonviolent existence."

"Except for the letter bomb," she reminded him.

"I told you, that was a fluke."

"Well, just in case flukes come in pairs, I've parked the car directly in front of the hospital door. I'll keep guard while the orderly pushes you to the car."

"Forget the wheelchair. I'm covered in bruises and I have a king-size headache, but my back is cured."

"Cured? Are you sure?"

"See?" He twisted his body back and forth to demonstrate. "Colliding with that car fixed my back."

"That's wonderful," she said. She chewed on her bottom lip. "But that doesn't change a thing. Your life is still in danger."

"Coming from you, I'm worried. Just tell me you're not going to flip me again."

"I'm serious. Listen, this job means a lot to me. My last job...well, things didn't go as well as they should and..."

"Is that the one where you lost a client?"

"Dogs aren't exactly my cup of tea."

"A dog?" He looked at her, incredulous. "Your last client was a dog?"

She nodded. "Someone was trying to kidnap him and unfortunately succeeded. But I'm not trained to protect dogs. I'm trained to protect people. You, Rick. I can protect you."

"I told you before, I'm not sure I even need protecting. You said this man had a gun. Did you actually see it?"

"Well, no, but...he's stalking you. I know he is."

Rick raked his fingers through his hair. Jack was proving to be more dangerous than any possible stalker—and her nearly killing him twice had nothing to do with it. He couldn't seem to form a cohesive thought when she was around. And since sampling those sweet-tasting lips of hers, he had suddenly become obsessed with the idea of helping himself to seconds.

"Please?" she pleaded, placing a hand on his arm, a hand that had driven him wild the night before, and threatened to drive him wild again. "Let me get you another bodyguard. Maybe Tiny Tim's available. He's six foot ten and weighs over three hundred..."

Nearly drowning in her luminous blue eyes, he prayed to God that a nurse—someone, anyone— would come through that door before he was tempted to do something about those lonely looking lips of hers. "Does Tiny Tim know martial arts?"

She nodded. "He even has a black belt."

"Then I'll pass. I don't want to be on the receiving end of anything Tiny might dish out."

She dropped her hand to her side. "Then let me stay for a couple more days. A week. What could it hurt? If after that time you're still convinced no one's out to get you, I'll leave."

There were probably a hundred reasons why he shouldn't let her stay, maybe even a thousand, but for the life of him, he couldn't think of a single one. His mind was clouded by the soft look in her eyes and the sweet nearness of her lips.

Dammit, if he ever did kiss her again, he'd be inclined to hold on to her forever. And *that* was definitely a bad idea. He had work to do. Work with a capital W.

"I don't know if I can survive a week of you trying to save my life." He meant it as a joke, almost. But judging from the way she wrinkled that cute little nose of hers, she took him seriously.

"I guess I've been a bit overzealous," she admitted.

He arched an eyebrow. Now they were getting somewhere. "A bit?"

"I didn't want to blow this job. After what happened to the poodle..." Her voice grew husky, but instead of giving in to tears like he expected, she lifted her chin and boldly met his gaze, her eyes shining with determination. "I promise from now on things will be different. At least let me secure the cabin. There're things you can do to protect yourself and—"

He raised his arms in full surrender. "Okay, okay." The words were out before he could stop himself, but immediately he regretted them. He'd just made a grave mistake, he was convinced of it. He'd already lost another full day of work, and he couldn't afford any more distractions. And if Jack was anything, she was definitely distracting. Especially when she flashed one of those beguiling smiles of hers. "One week," he added.

Her smile brightened. "You won't be sorry."

He was already sorry.

She turned toward the door, then stopped. "One more thing..." She faced him. "The S. J. Spade Agency forbids any personal involvement with clients. That means from now on, everything must be strictly business between us. No more..."

He looked her over boldly. "Kisses?"

She nodded, and her lips quivered as if the word itself was now forbidden.

"No problem," he said. By bringing this out in the open, she made it all that much easier to face a few hard facts. He didn't have time for such non-sense—no matter how tempting her lips might be. Time was running out; if he didn't finish the computer program in thirty days, he'd miss the production deadline and a year of hard work would go down the tubes.

"Last night..." It wasn't often that he bothered with explanations. Certainly, he'd never had to explain a kiss. "I...guess the shock of being flipped to the floor in the middle of the night made me...crazy."

Actually, it was seeing her in that sexy T-shirt that had made him crazy. Even now, he could recall with startling clarity the way the shirt molded against her softly rounded breasts and hips, showing off those shapely legs of hers. The memory was so real to him, he began to physically ache, just as he had last night when she ran her hands up and down his body.

His jaw tight, he lifted his foot to the chair to tie his shoe. The shoelace snapped in his hand and, disgusted, he dropped his foot to the floor.

She gave a tentative smile and he wondered if she thought he was mad at her. Hell, what had happened wasn't *entirely* her fault.

"Shock can do strange things to people," she agreed.

"So they say." He watched her face. "I just want you to know nothing like it will happen again." He hoped to see disappointment register in her eyes, and his spirits dropped when he saw nothing of the kind. If anything, he saw relief. "I have work to do," he added curtly. The least she could do was *act* disappointed.

"Yes, yes, work," she said, acting businesslike. "And don't you worry about a thing. You won't even know I'm here." She spun around and opened the door. "All clear," she said.

She stood guard by the reception desk while he signed the release papers.

"I have to stop at the men's room," he said, heading across the lobby.

"Wait!" She pushed ahead of him, knocked on the rest room door and, when no one answered, pushed her way inside. "All clear," she announced again, flashing him yet another one of her heart-stopping smiles.

"Are you coming in?" he asked. He wouldn't put it past her.

"Don't you worry about a thing," she said. "I'll be right outside the door."

Moments later, he stood in front of the double glass doors leading outside as she had instructed, watching her check out his Blazer. She was all over it. She even crawled underneath it. A soldier checking for land mines couldn't have been more diligent. She was thorough, no doubt about it. Just as she had been thorough in checking him out for injuries.

Even now, he could feel her soft, gentle hands running up and down his spine, his legs, his…

Dammit! He was doing it again. Thinking thoughts that distracted him from his work.

Tearing his gaze away from her, he slipped on his sunglasses and scanned the surrounding area. Suddenly, he found himself seeing things he'd never before noticed. Like the black sedan across the street, and the man loitering outside the Mexican restaurant. Like the old woman walking with a cane.

He shook his head. It was crazy. Not only was he obsessed with his bodyguard, he was fast becoming paranoid. Everyone and everything suddenly seemed like a threat.

He glared at Jack. Now she'd done it, really done it to him! It wasn't enough that she'd twice tried to kill him, and taunted him with that sexy body of hers. No, she had to go and mess up his brain.

Well, enough was enough. No one was out to get him. Not if he had anything to say about it!

She motioned to him to join her, her hand on the weapon beneath her vest.

He balled his hands by his sides. It was about time. Now maybe they could finish their business in town and return to the cabin. With a little luck, he might still be able to salvage the day and get some work done.

He sure as hell didn't need any more distractions, especially not from a bold, know-it-all lady-P.I.-in-training bodyguard whose smile could melt the Arctic ice cap if she put her mind to it.

10

RICK GREW MORE IMPATIENT by the minute. It was already three in the afternoon, and they still hadn't started back to the cabin.

It was taking them twice as long as he'd expected to get his prescription filled, partly because of the long line, but mainly because Jack insisted upon checking every square inch of the damn drugstore before allowing him to stand in line.

"I'm telling you, I don't need to get my prescription filled," he grumbled. "My back no longer hurts." Just his head and his legs and his shoulder and his...

"What if your back starts hurting in the middle of the night?" she asked, staring at the man who had just walked through the front door. Fortunately, he turned out to be the husband of the cashier. Fortunately, because Rick didn't think he could endure another one of Jack's interrogations.

She had already queried everyone in line to find out what they were doing there. Not a good idea. People with ailments loved to talk about them, and he had learned more about arthritis, diabetes and baldness that afternoon than he ever cared to know.

"When did baldness become a disease?" he whispered in Jack's ear, after a bald-pated man had described in great detail what it was like to suffer the heartbreak of alopecia.

She shrugged. "I thought everything that's contagious was a disease."

"Contag—" Rick's hand flew to his own thick hair before the amusement in her eyes gave her away. "Thanks a lot," he muttered.

The long wait in line wasn't the least of it. When he went to pay for the pain pills and shoelaces with his credit card, Jack whipped the card out of his hand. "You can't use your credit cards, or even your ATM card. These can be tracked by computer. You may as well broadcast your whereabouts on the news."

"So how am I supposed to pay?"

"Use my card." She handed the youthful clerk the credit card issued to all of the Spade agents for just such occasions. "It'll be added to your bill."

After leaving the drugstore, Jacquie insisted upon stopping at the hardware store and purchasing an assortment of locks. It meant more security checks, more customer stories—this time regarding break-ins and robberies—and more wasted time.

By the time they left the hardware store laden with packages, Rick was in a bad mood. He no longer had a single headache; he had a whole series of them, starting at the top of his head and throbbing in a trail to his jawbone.

Though the Blazer had been within sight the whole time they shopped, Jack still checked it over carefully before allowing him anywhere near it. By the time he was seated inside and she had taken her place behind the steering wheel, he was tempted, more than tempted, to wring her pretty little neck.

Apparently oblivious to his rotten mood—or how far she had pushed his patience—she acted as if everything was perfectly normal. "I need to ask you some questions. It's part of my job." She glanced at him. "We can do it while traveling or wait until we get to the cabin."

"Just get it over with," he growled. Once he was back at the cabin, he planned to lock himself into his bedroom with his laptop and not put his head outside the door until morning.

"Do you mind if I record your answers? That way I can fill in the forms later."

"Whatever. Just get it over with."

She reached into her backpack, dug out her tape recorder and flipped it on. She then pulled out of the parking lot, watching the rearview mirror for any cars that might be following.

"I need to know your daily routine. What time you get up. Go to bed. That kind of thing."

"I get up at six and go to bed when I'm tired, generally around midnight."

"What do you do when you get up?"

"Grab a cup of coffee, shower and shave, then head for my desk."

"That's it?"

"Basically, yeah."

"How often do you leave the cabin? On average."

"When we get back, I don't intend to leave the

cabin until I've completed my program. Except perhaps to take a jog and clear the brain."

"Jogging's out," she said. "Unless you stay inside and jog in place."

"If the president of the United States can jog, then so can I."

"The president has a whole team of Secret Service men watching his every move. I'm only one person. No outside jogs."

"Are you always this bossy?"

"Are you always this stubborn?"

He shrugged and laid his head back on the headrest. "What else do you want to know about me?"

Glancing continually at the rearview mirror, she proceeded to ask him the usual questions—date and place of birth, how long he'd been working for Stanwicke and Lanswell, where he went to school. "Any birthmarks or tattoos?"

"You could probably answer that question better than I can," he said.

Blushing at the memory of running her hands up and down his body, she quickly changed the subject. "What about family? Parents? Siblings?"

"My father's dead, and my mother lives in Houston with my sister and her husband."

"I need the names of everyone who knows you're here in Falcon Heights."

"That's easy. My boss, Russ Parker, is the only one who knows my whereabouts. It's his cabin."

"Are you sure? None of the other employees know? Your mother?"

"Russ is the only one who knows. That's the way he wanted it."

"Smart man." Or maybe just cunning. Maybe the plan was to get Rick isolated somewhere, before a second attempt was made on his life. "Have you used any credit cards since leaving San Francisco? Your gas card?"

"I filled up on the way here, and yes, I used a credit card."

She sighed. "That means you've left an electronic trail. Parker might not be the only one who knows you're here."

"I'm telling you, no one cares where I am."

"Someone cares," she said, eyeing the rearview mirror.

"Who?"

"The person or persons in that car behind us."

The black sedan had been tailing them since they'd left the parking lot, and it was still following them, even though she'd made several turns in an effort to lose it.

Rick turned to stare out the back window. "I think I saw that same black sedan in town."

"Are you able to make out the license plate?" she asked, braking at the stop sign.

"No, it's too far away."

"All right." She checked for oncoming traffic. "Hold on." She sped away from the intersection, made a fast right and a fast left, her tires squealing. It wasn't easy to lose a tail in a town as small as Falcon Heights, especially driving a red car. "Do you know how to reach the cabin from the other direction?"

"I'm not sure." Rick reached in the glove compartment and pulled out a map.

The winding road narrowed dangerously and she was forced to slow down. "When we go around this next turn, look back and see if you see the sedan."

Rick turned in his seat. "No, the coast is clear."

She sighed with relief and pulled off the road onto a scenic-lookout area. Now if they could just figure out another route to the cabin...

Rick continued to study the map. "It looks like we're out of luck. The dirt road dead-ends about a half mile beyond the cabin. There's no other way in."

"I think we should stay somewhere else tonight."

"I can't do that. My computer is at the cabin. My files."

"We'll hire someone to go back to the cabin for you."

"I can't take a chance on someone sabotaging my work. Take me back. If someone's following, let them follow."

"Bad idea, Rick. Besides, I'm in charge and I say the cabin is too dangerous."

"I'm your boss and I say we're going back!" They glared at each other.

"All right," she said, throwing the car into gear. "Have it your own way. But don't say I didn't warn you!"

Neither spoke on the drive back, but tension between them was so taut it almost depleted the cab of air. Every crossroad required extra vigilance, every car posed a potential threat until it was close enough to identify.

They made it all the way back to the cabin without mishap. "Stay here," she said.

"Jack...I know this is your job...but be careful, you hear?"

The concern on his face, in his eyes, momentarily took her breath away. It was hard to recall anyone ever being that concerned about her welfare. "Would you be telling me to be careful if I was six foot ten and weighed three hundred pounds?"

"Probably not," he said honestly. "So call me a chauvinist."

"Keep the door locked and your head down." She quickly scanned the area for tire marks or footprints. She then checked the nearly invisible threads she'd attached to the top of the door and at each window. Her method wasn't exactly high-tech, but it served its purpose. She was a hundred percent certain that no one had entered the cabin while they were in town.

THE FOLLOWING MORNING, Jacquie rose just after seven. Already she could hear Rick moving around downstairs. She peered through the window of her room and was almost blinded by the bright morning sun. Everything looked perfectly calm and serene outside.

She followed the rich smell of freshly brewed coffee down the stairs and into the kitchen. Rick was already at his desk, working on his laptop computer. He'd worked practically nonstop since they'd arrived home yesterday and she wondered if he'd gotten any sleep.

"Good morning," she called.

"Good morning." His voice sounded gravelly.

She filled her cup and leaned against the doorjamb, studying him. The grim determination on his face reminded her of her father when he worked. As a child, she'd learned that any attempts to capture her father's attention at such times ended in failure. "You just keep working and don't worry about me. You won't even know I'm here."

He grunted in acknowledgment, but his fingers kept pounding on the keys. Leaving him to work undisturbed she turned and walked back into the kitchen.

After helping herself to cornflakes and toast, Jacquie showered and dressed, then slipped quietly outside to check out the property.

Blue jays squawked in protest as she drew near, chipmunks ran for cover, but otherwise, all was quiet.

After an hour or so, she returned to the cabin, letting herself in quietly so as not to disturb Rick.

She spent the remainder of the morning conducting a methodical check of each room. One of the requirements of her job was to fill out a building-security checklist.

She had installed the extra locks on the door and windows after returning to the cabin yesterday. All that male influence in her childhood had paid off. She was almost as handy with tools as her brother Casey, who owned a national chain of hardware stores.

Still, no lock could take the place of a good alarm system.

She took special care in checking out Rick's bedroom. She could hardly take her eyes off the unmade bed. Judging by the tangle of sheets and blankets, Rick was a restless sleeper.

Running her fingers over his pillow, she caught a whiff of his aftershave, and the way her heart began to pound, she could have played percussion for a rap band.

Turning abruptly, she forced herself to concentrate on the clipboard in her hand and the form that was yet to be filled out. Heaving a sigh, she wrote in the space allotted for comments "the bedroom is a dangerous place."

Rick was still working away on his computer when she decided to break for lunch. "Do you mind if I make a sandwich or something?" she called from the kitchen.

"Help yourself," he replied.

"Are you hungry?"

The question seemed to surprise him, as if eating was the furthest thing from his mind. "I don't eat when I'm working."

Shrugging to herself, she pulled a package of bacon and a tomato out of the refrigerator. She arranged the bacon in a frying pan, and soon the kitchen was filled with a delicious savory smell.

"All right, you talked me into it."

Unaware that he stood directly behind her, she jumped at the sound of his voice, the knife flying out of her hand and falling to the floor with a clatter.

She spun around to face him, her back pressed against the counter for support. It was hard to know what annoyed her more—Rick sneaking up on her or the fact that she hadn't heard him enter the kitchen. *Thou shalt stay alert. Another commandment bites the dust.*

"You scared me."

"Sorry. But blame it on the smell of bacon. I couldn't resist." He picked up a crisp piece and popped it into his mouth.

She picked up the knife off the floor and tossed it into the sink. Arranging a sandwich on a plate, she handed it to him. His fingers touched hers as he took the plate, and a bolt of electricity shot through her.

"Thanks," he said, giving no clue as to whether or not he'd noticed the same jolt. He grabbed two cans of soda out of the refrigerator and set one on the counter for her.

Straddling a bar stool in front of the counter that divided the kitchen from the dining area, he hungrily attacked his sandwich.

She sat on the stool next to his. "How's the work going?"

"Not good. There's a problem with the program that I can't seem to fix. I've been working on this same problem for nearly two months now, and I'm no closer to solving it today than I was back then."

She studied his profile. He looked worried, or at least the lines crinkling the corner of his eyes were more noticeable. "Maybe you're trying too hard. Sometimes it helps to take a rest from a problem. You know, let the subconscious take over."

"I don't think that would work in this case. Uninterrupted concentration is the key. Besides, I never had much luck with my subconscious."

"The trick is to concentrate on something else completely. Sometimes you get an idea when you least expect it. Like in the shower."

A half smile crossed his face and he regarded her with a speculative gaze. "Is that where you get your ideas? In the shower?"

"Sometimes," she said, feeling her face grow warm. She lifted the can of soda and held it next to her burning cheek. What was the matter with her? Having three brothers, she could generally talk to men about anything. In fact, before meeting Rick, she couldn't remember the last time she'd blushed. Or stammered. Or even felt her pulse race.

She took a sip of the cold beverage and set the can on the counter. "Mostly I get my ideas when I'm doing something I really enjoy, like shopping or walking along the beach."

"I haven't taken time off in I can't remember how long," he said. "Too much work to do."

She nibbled her sandwich slowly, wishing with her all heart she'd heard a note of regret—something—in his voice that told her he wanted more out of life than to keep his nose to the grindstone.

As Aunt Samantha liked to say, it was déjà vu all over again. Jacquie had been maybe eight or nine, still too young to question life, when she first remembered her father saying almost the exact same words to her. *Run along and play, Jacquie, I've got work to do.* As she grew older, her needs changed, but his excuse for not participating in her life remained constant.

Eventually, she'd stopped asking her father to do anything with her, and never even mentioned her high school graduation to him out of fear of being disappointed yet again if he didn't show up. Secretly, she'd hoped he'd show up unannounced, but he didn't, of course.

There was a time when she honestly thought she'd come to terms with her father's remoteness, but it turned out not to be true. That's why it hurt so much when he'd brought his ever-present attaché case to the hospital the day her mother lay on her deathbed.

It took Jacquie years to forgive him that transgression and even longer to accept the fact that wishing things were different didn't make them so. Her father was a workaholic and, obviously, so was Rick Westley.

Rick finished his sandwich and, without lingering so much as a moment, stood. "Well, back to the old grind."

"Yeah," she said, feeling oddly depressed. "Back to work."

She cleaned up the kitchen and wandered into the living room. She felt restless and out of sorts. This sitting around waiting for something to happen was not her style.

If she had her way, she would drive back to San Francisco and interview everyone who knew Rick.

Maybe one of them would lead to the person or persons responsible for the mail bomb. Better yet, she'd track down Rick's stalker herself and personally escort him to the nearest police department.

Rick insisted he had no enemies, but obviously that wasn't true. Whether or not he wanted to admit it, somebody wanted him dead. She was willing to bet on it.

She sat on the couch next to the window and opened the draperies a crack. From where she sat, she could see the dirt road through the trees. She thumbed through a magazine, her nerves on edge. She tried to ignore Rick, but her eyes seemed to have a mind of their own. No matter how hard she tried to focus on the glossy pages, she found herself seeking him out.

Even dressed in a pair of faded jeans and an old flannel shirt, he was the sexiest man she'd ever met. And could he ever kiss!

Okay, so he claimed he'd been out of his head when he kissed her, which was probably his way of telling her that it didn't mean a thing.

Well, his kisses might not have meant anything to him, but they sure had done a number on her. She shuddered to think of the havoc to her senses had he actually *meant* to kiss her.

As it was, her mouth still burned with the feel of his lips, her body tingled as if she'd stuck her finger into an electrical outlet.

She tossed the magazine aside. Just what she needed. A full-fledged lust attack.

Maybe she'd been working too hard. This bodyguard business was stressful. Maybe she would ask her aunt for some time off before she took another assignment. Time off to do…what?

She hadn't dated much lately. Heck, she hadn't been on an honest-to-goodness date in months. Her only company had been that spoiled pooch, Lord Byron. No wonder a self-absorbed workaholic like Rick Westley looked good.

It was a sobering thought and one she didn't want to think about. She also didn't want to think about how many of her aunt's commandments she had broken, thought of breaking or was close to breaking while guarding Rick Westley.

What she needed was a cup of hot tea. She stood, but before she reached the kitchen, something hit the living room window, hard!

he wings frantically when Jacquie tried to pick it up.

Without warning, the jay flew a few feet away from her to the pine at the lower edge of the small lot.

Perhaps it was waiting more to be done for the bird, Jacquie turned to find Rick on the porch

_____ **11** _____

JACQUIE SPUN AROUND and reached for her gun. "Drop to the floor!" A look of horror crossed Rick's face, but for once, he gave her no argument. Instead, he dove off his chair, hitting the floor with his hands spread in front of him.

Weapon in hand, she raced across the room. In her haste, she bumped the desk and sent his laptop flying. The computer fell to the floor with a crash.

Her back flat against the wall, gun held up, she moved the draperies and glanced out the window. Nothing.

She darted to the door. "Stay where you are," she cried. Outside, she stood on the porch and scanned the area.

At first she saw nothing. Then a slight movement caught her eye. A blue jay lay on the ground, its wings fluttering. Sighing in relief, she stuck her gun into its holster and hurried down the steps.

"There, there, little fellow." Stopping a few feet away from the trembling bird, she stooped and held out her hand. The bird appeared to be stunned, but as far as she could tell, its wings weren't broken.

Keeping her distance, she talked to the jay in a soothing voice for a minute, but the bird flapped its wings frantically when Jacquie tried to move closer.

Without warning, the jay flew to a nearby bush. From the top of a pine came the encouraging cry of another jay.

Since there was nothing more to be done for the bird, Jacquie turned, to find Rick on the porch watching her. "I told you to stay inside."

His dark eyes sought hers. "I was worried about you."

"Why?" she snapped. "Because I'm a woman and you don't think I can handle myself?"

"I'm sorry." He looked genuinely apologetic, and she knew it wouldn't take much for her to melt on the spot. "I didn't mean that the way it sounded."

Her mouth tightened. With fingers shoved into the back pockets of her jeans, she kicked a pinecone with the toe of her sneaker. It wasn't like her to be so defensive. The truth was, she liked him being concerned about her welfare. Liked it a lot. But his concern only made her job that much more difficult to do.

She narrowed her eyes. "If I'm going to work for you, we need to get something straight. I'm a trained professional and it's my job to watch out for your safety. Not the other way around."

She stomped up the steps to the porch and started past him, but he stopped her, his hand on her arm. "I said I was sorry."

She lifted her chin. Their eyes locked for a moment before he released her. Her trembling knees threatened to fail her.

She waited for him to enter the cabin, and after a quick look around, followed him inside, locking the door behind her.

He picked his laptop off the floor and began to check it out.

She waited, dreading the verdict. "Is it okay?" she asked, her mouth dry.

At first he didn't answer her. He just kept clicking the mouse. Finally, he cursed beneath his breath. He turned the computer off, then rebooted. After a while, he flipped the switch off and closed the lid. "It's not working."

It was the last thing she wanted to hear. She felt terrible. All she'd done since arriving in Falcon Heights was cause him trouble. "I'm sorry, Rick. I don't know what to say."

His face grim, he packed the computer into a black carrying case. "I'm going into town to use the phone. I'll have my boss overnight me another computer."

Never one to cry over spilled milk, she felt perilously close to shedding tears over a smashed computer. *Thou shalt not show emotion on the job.*

Jacquie blinked back the moisture in her eyes and swallowed hard. "I feel absolutely terrible."

"Yeah, well, if I hurry, my boss will still have time to ship one out today." He grabbed his car keys and headed for the door.

Chasing after him, she shouted, "Wait!"

NEITHER OF THEM uttered a word on their way to the village. Rick drove, keeping his eyes on the road the whole time. Much to Jacquie's relief, they didn't see another car until they turned onto the main highway leading into town.

Rick pulled in at a grocery store and stopped in front of a row of phone booths. It was not a safe spot. Anyone could be hiding in the crowded parking lot, watching them, taking aim.

Shielding him with her own body, Jacquie stood guard. She searched the sea of parked cars for the black sedan, studied the shoppers pushing carts filled with grocery bags. So far, there was no sign of the man in the black leather jacket.

Nonetheless, she couldn't shake the feeling they were being watched.

After a brief conversation, Rick hung up the phone. "It's settled," he said. "I should receive another laptop by this time tomorrow." He glanced around. "What do you say we grab something to eat before heading back?"

"Well..." A passing car suddenly slowed down. Her hand beneath her vest, she prepared to draw her gun. The car pulled into an empty space and two women emerged. Jacquie dropped her arm to her side.

"Who's the workaholic now?" Without waiting for an answer, he cupped her elbow and steered her to the Italian restaurant at the end of the shopping mall, diagonally across from the grocery store.

As they waited to be seated, he leaned over and whispered in her ear, "Don't tell me restaurants are dangerous, too." His breath, warm against her flesh, made her feel slightly giddy.

"Only if you're a member of the Mafia," she

whispered back, only half joking. Restaurants weren't the only dangerous places for members of the Mob; one notable Mafia member had been shot in a barbershop.

"We'll take the booth in back," she told the maître d'. "Away from the window."

Only two other couples occupied the restaurant, neither of them showing any particular interest in her and Rick.

Unwilling to take even the slightest chance with his safety, she opted for the seat facing the door. Rick sat opposite her, picked up the menu and studied it intently.

She barely glanced at her own menu. She was too busy watching the entryway. "Rick, I'm really sorry about your computer." She shifted her gaze to meet his. "If you give me a copy of the bill, I'll be happy to reimburse you—"

"That won't be necessary." He closed the menu and reached for the wine list. "The company will take care of any repairs."

"Did you lose much work?"

"Not much. I've learned from experience that it pays to have an efficient backup system."

She folded her hands together and rested her chin on them. "This might be a blessing in disguise, you know? Taking a day or two off work. It might give you a whole new perspective. Maybe it'll help you solve the problem you're having. The one you said you've been working on for the last two months."

He set the wine list on the table. "It's more likely to give me an ulcer."

Laughter floated from the booth across the way and Jacquie looked up sharply.

Rick watched her. "They're just having a good time," he said.

Feeling foolish, she felt compelled to explain. She didn't want him to think her nervousness had anything to do with him, personally. "The man who shot Governor Wallace was photographed smiling up to the moment he fired his gun."

Rick lifted a dark brow, but before he had a chance to reply, the waiter walked over to their table to take their order.

Afterward, Jacquie excused herself. The telephone was by the front door and offered her a full view of the restaurant. She could call the office without letting down her guard.

Mark answered on the second ring. "S. J. Spade Insurance Agency."

"It's me, Jack. I'm just checking in."

"Jack! Your aunt's been waiting to hear from you. The lawsuit—"

She felt her stomach muscles tighten. "Don't tell me there's another problem."

"No, nothing like that. In fact, it's good news."

Another couple walked into the restaurant and Jacquie looked them over carefully before deciding they were harmless. "I could use some good news along about now."

"Lord Byron has been found."

"What?"

"It's true."

"Is he okay?"

Mark hesitated. "Let's just say he's no longer the reigning king of Don Juans."

"What?" Jacquie couldn't believe her ears. "Are you saying the kidnappers had him fixed?"

"Pretty amazing, huh? The old lady is livid, but the animal activists are singing your praises."

Jacquie laughed at the news. "I guess there're worse fates than having animal activists on your side."

"I knew you'd be relieved."

"You'll never know how much. Listen…has there been any news on the letter bomb? Any arrests?"

"Not that I know of. Why?"

"Do me a favor. Call the police department and find out if there're any new leads."

Mark sighed. "Oh, dear. Samantha won't like this."

"I know, I know." *Thou shalt not meddle with police investigations.* "Mark, please, this is important."

"So is my job."

"I'll make it up to you. I promise."

Mark hesitated, but finally relented, as Jacquie knew he would. "All right. But it's going to cost you. I want your secret recipe for beef Wellington."

Jacquie gritted her teeth. Trust Mark to drive a hard bargain. "It's yours."

"In that case, I'll see what I can do."

"Thanks." She hung up. Rick looked up as she approached the table. "Good news?" he asked. It wasn't until he asked the question that she realized she was smiling.

"They found Lord Byron."

"That's great," Rick said. "Is he okay?"

"Yeah, except the kidnappers had him fixed." She opened up her menu. "What did I tell you? You're perfectly safe with me."

IT WAS DARK by the time they left the restaurant and Jacquie finished checking out the Blazer. She'd insisted Rick stand away from the car during her inspection. Now she signaled to him to join her. The parking lot was half-empty, though traffic was heavy as tourists driving oversize motor homes began to arrive in town for the weekend.

Just as Rick reached the car, a bright flash caught the corner of her eye. Shoving down hard on his shoulders, she struck the back of his knees with her own, reducing his height to better shield him.

"What the—"

"Shhh." Another light caught her eye, and she realized it was a fireball zipping across the sky. Releasing him, she backed up. "Oh, look! It's the Perseid meteor shower." No sooner were the words out of her mouth than another fireball streaked toward the horizon.

Rick looked at her oddly. "You pushed me down because of a meteor shower?"

"I didn't want you to miss it," she said, not willing to admit she'd overreacted. Two fiery balls streaked past Orion's sword and she clapped her hands in delight.

"Wow!" Rick said. "Was that for real?"

She laughed. "What did I tell you? You can only see it in August. Tonight is supposed to be the best night for viewing."

"You said the meteor shower can be seen every August?" He looked surprised.

"It's hard to see in the city," she said. "With all the lights."

"What a pity." He shifted his gaze to her face. "I would never have pegged you for a stargazer. You're full of surprises, aren't you?"

The way he looked at her nearly took her breath away. "If you want to know the truth, you don't know Jack about me."

He chuckled softly. "Is that so? Maybe it's time I did."

His face looked perfectly composed, but his velvety voice and burning eyes confirmed what she already suspected. Without his computer to keep him occupied, the man could be dangerous.

Judging by the way he held her in his gaze, he had a mind to work over her body with the same diligence that made him a workaholic, and once started, he might never stop. The thought was as thrilling as it was...well...thrilling!

He lifted his hand to her cheek and she barely had the presence of mind to push it away. "Like I told you before, it's against company policy for employees to fraternize with clients."

"You have no worry in that regard," he said. "I have a little bit more than fraternizing on my mind."

Now this was getting interesting. *Mighty* interesting. Mentally filing it in the getting-to-know-the-client file, she decided to ask for details. You could tell a lot about a man by how he made love.

Unfortunately, before she had a chance to satisfy her curiosity, she noticed a pickup heading down the street with its headlights off.

"Get in the car," she said. Though she doubted anyone would be so foolish as to harm Rick in the middle of town, she wasn't about to take unnecessary chances. Hand on her gun, she blocked his body with her own until the pickup turned into the gas station at the corner. Another false alarm.

She climbed into the car. With her hand on the back of her neck, she moved her head back and forth to work out the soreness between her shoulder blades.

They made the trip back to the cabin without mishap, though Rick seemed determined to get to know her on a more personal level. The way he questioned her about her childhood, her schooling and even the kind of music she liked, you'd think he had a mental getting-to-know-you file of his own.

"I like country music," she said, knowing full well she should put a stop to this. An agent was not supposed to reveal personal information to a client.

"Brothers? Sisters?"

"Three brothers. All younger than me." And every one of them successful in whatever he did. Though she was happy for them, it sure didn't make her life any easier. She hated the fact that out of the four of them, she was the only one to drop out of school, not once but several times.

"What do your parents do?"

"My father is a lawyer and my mother..." Even now it pained her to say it. "My mother's dead."

"I'm sorry."

"She was a mystery writer. Perhaps you've heard of her? Her pseudonym was J. T. Connors."

"J. T. Connors was your mother? I don't believe it. Really?"

She laughed at his expression. "Don't tell me you're a mystery reader."

"I'm afraid I don't have time to read for pleasure. But everyone's heard of J. T. Connors. What do you know? Next you'll be telling me that your father is Jason Summers, the great criminal lawyer."

No, she would not tell him that. Even though it just happened to be true.

"What about you?" she asked, anxious to change the subject. "Why the fascination with computers?"

Once the subject turned to computers, his whole demeanor changed. It was as if nothing else existed.

"When I was a kid, I used to watch my dad at work. He had a little fix-it shop and he was always taking things apart, putting them back together. Sometimes he'd let me help him." Rick fell silent for a moment, as if to enjoy some long-ago memory. "When he repaired something, it was better than the day it had been bought new."

The thought of Rick as a little boy, helping his

father, brought a squeezing pain to Jacquie's chest. She'd never been allowed to help her parents or feel that she had a place in their work-oriented lives. But she did recall the countless times she had begged her parents to come outside with her for no other reason than to watch the sunset, or a spider spinning a web. Nothing really earth-shattering. Just little everyday things that were anything but ordinary if shared with a loved one.

She could still hear her father's voice. *I'll be there in a minute. Run along now....* Could still recall with crystal-clear clarity her mother's usual response. *Just as soon as I finish this chapter.*

Promises made in good faith were soon forgotten when work intervened. That was the price Jacquie had paid for having parents who were so successful. It was one of the reasons she had spent so much of her childhood alone.

Now she wished with all her heart that she had been the kind of child to throw temper tantrums when she didn't get her own way. Maybe then she could look at a sunset or a meteor shower without feeling regret at having never shared the memory with those she loved most.

"It was the saddest day of his life when my father finally closed down his shop."

She looked up at him. "Why did he?"

"It was no longer cost-effective to fix appliances. It became cheaper to buy new ones."

She liked that Rick empathized with his father. Some might be inclined to think his father old-fashioned, but Rick apparently didn't.

She felt so close to him that, oddly enough, she

lost track of time and hardly noticed the drive back to the cabin. She was surprised when Rick pulled off the dirt road and parked next to her Toyota. She could have sworn they had only just left the town.

After checking to make sure she could grab her gun if she needed to, she climbed out of the car, straining her ears against the cacophony of croaking frogs. Not even the bright stars overhead seemed to penetrate the dark woods, which was both a blessing and curse.

She heard the door open on the driver's side. "Stay where you are," she ordered. Hands on the car, she felt her way around the front, and bumped into him.

She took a deep breath. "I told you to stay where you were. Don't you listen to anything I say?"

He slipped his arms around her waist. "I heard what you said about it being strictly business between us. But I'm having a hell of a time keeping my hands off you."

Her heart thudded against her ribs. "Rick, I…we…I told you, it's strictly forbidden."

"You're not going to be my bodyguard forever," he said.

"Rick, please, we shouldn't be standing out here. The killing zone—"

He pulled her close, and every sensible thought in her head disappeared in a cloud of masculine presence. No longer able to form a sensible thought, she raised herself on tiptoes to take whatever bliss he offered.

His lips felt like heaven even before she folded her arms around his neck to deepen the kiss. *He* felt like heaven, and when at last he pulled his mouth away, it felt as if he'd taken a little piece of her with him.

"And I'm not going to be working on this damn program forever," he whispered.

The mention of work didn't cool her ardor, not this time. It only made her want to explore the subject in search of some possibility she'd previously overlooked. Maybe he could change, wanted to change, if only given enough incentive.

"If it's not this program, it'll be another." It was a question more than a statement, and she held her breath, waiting for his response.

It was too dark to see his face, but she sensed his confusion. "I don't understand. Are you saying that because I'm a computer programmer, I can't have a life?"

"It wouldn't matter what profession you were in. You're a workaholic. You said it yourself."

"Lots of workaholics get married, have children...."

Something in his voice, some unwillingness to change, perhaps, made her pull away. "I know." Suddenly she felt cold. "I'm one of those children." She shivered and stuck her hands in the pockets of her jacket.

It was dangerous to be standing outside like this. Dangerous for more reasons than she cared to name. "We better go inside."

12

JACQUIE ROSE EARLY the next morning and headed
for the shower. It was still dark when she tiptoed
up the stairs to the loft, but she held her breath until she reached the safety of her room. Quickly, she
dressed in a pair of khaki shorts and a knit top,
then reached into her duffel bag for her hairbrush.

All right, so she'd blown it. She'd given in to a
moment of weakness and kissed her client. Again!
That didn't mean she couldn't do her job. Or even
that she had let her aunt down. It wasn't as if she'd
broken the *real* commandments.

Pulling the brush through her wet hair, she
made a plan. When she faced Rick that morning,
she would simply act as if nothing had happened.
Denial was a legitimate coping device. So, for that
matter, was dropping out of sight.

She tossed the hairbrush onto the bed and
reached for her lipstick. She stopped herself. *Jack
Summers, you are a bodyguard. Now start acting like
one!*

Wearing no lipstick, head held high, shoulders
back, she eyed herself in the mirror. Wouldn't you
know it?

Even in the dim glow of the overhead electric
light, her skin was a healthy pink color that no
amount of makeup could have achieved. Even her

eyes sparkled, the blue bright as the sky, the whites clear as freshly fallen snow. Obviously, the clean mountain air agreed with her. *And that's all it is! Just plain, old-fashioned air.*

When she heard Rick moving around downstairs, her heart skipped a beat. This brought yet more color to her cheeks, more sparkle to her eyes. She chewed her lip and pulled out her gun. That did it. Now she looked like a bodyguard who meant business. Just let anyone suggest otherwise!

Forcing her face into a serious demeanor, she marched downstairs.

She might have believed her own act had Rick not looked at her with one of those heart-stopping, pulse-kicking smiles of his.

She almost blew it by smiling back. Catching herself just in time, she wrinkled her forehead in what she hoped was a scowl that conveyed the appropriate message: *touch me and you're dead, buster!*

Judging by the way the smile quickly died on his face, it worked. "I hope you aren't planning to use that thing on me."

Her mind whirled in confusion before it occurred to her that he was referring to the gun pointed straight at his manhood.

She lowered her arm and backed toward the door. "Not a chance," she muttered. "I'm, uh, going to check outside."

"Don't you want some coffee first?"

"No, I don't!" she snapped. "And I'd appreciate it if you would stop interfering with my work."

He arched a dark brow. "But—"

She quickly let herself outside, slamming the

door after her. Surprised to find herself shaking, she slid the gun into her shoulder holster and surveyed the surrounding area before leaving the porch. Now *that* was how a professional conducted herself.

The air was clear and brisk, but already rays of golden sunshine bathed the uppermost parts of the shimmering, tall pines. A determined woodpecker hammered against a tree trunk, ignoring the noisy jays swooping in and out of the branches overhead.

Breathing in the crisp mountain air, she circled the cabin. Senses alert, she scanned the area, but no matter how much she tried to keep her mind on the task at hand, she couldn't stop thinking of Rick and the forbidden kiss they had shared beneath a magical star-studded sky.

She shivered involuntarily and picked up her pace in a desperate effort to dispel the urge to turn back and rush into his arms.

She had no intention of returning to the cabin until she had herself fully under control. All right, halfway under control. She could manage at least that much.

It took nearly an hour before her pulse was anywhere near back to normal and another hour before she could look at the cabin without her knees starting to wobble. Even then she wasn't certain she could face Rick.

The tantalizing smell of bacon and freshly brewed coffee greeted her, along with Rick's rich baritone voice raised in song as, key in hand, she walked into the cabin. Few people could sing the national anthem, let alone sing it with such gusto.

She stood at the kitchen door and clapped her hands heartily when he finished. "Not bad."

"What do you mean, not bad?" He lifted a mesh basket out of a pan of water. "It's the only way to time an egg. But you have to sing at just the right tempo. It's all in the tempo."

"Tempo, huh?" She poured herself a cup of coffee and sat at the counter. "Now I know why my eggs are always on the rubbery side. Where'd you learn to cook?"

"My mother owned a restaurant. The customers were required to sing the national anthem after placing their orders. It was the only way my mother could time the eggs."

Jacquie laughed. "They never taught me that in cooking school."

"You went to cooking school?"

"For a while."

"What happened?"

"One of the chefs died of food poisoning. I decided I preferred a less dangerous occupation."

"And you think being a bodyguard is less dangerous?"

"No bodyguard on record ever died from eating liver pâté."

"I guess you have a point." He set two steaming plates on the counter and sat down opposite her.

"This looks wonderful," she said. The eggs had been timed to perfection and the bacon cooked to just the right crispness. She smiled but he didn't notice. He was too busy writing notes on a yellow pad, his plate untouched. "What time do we have to pick up your computer?"

"Deliveries don't arrive in town until four."

"Oh." She finished her breakfast in silence.

After a while, he cursed beneath his breath and abruptly left the table. Obviously, he was still unable to solve the problem with his program.

After breakfast, she found him pacing the living room restlessly, hands locked behind his back. He stopped midstep. "What do you say we go into town now? It's possible the UPS could arrive early."

"Not this early." It was only ten o'clock. Actually, she didn't want to go into town at all. It made protecting him that much more difficult. "I don't think it's a good idea to spend any more time in town than necessary."

He started to argue with her, but apparently thought better of it. He stared at his yellow pad for a moment before tossing it onto his desk and heading for the door. "I'm going for a walk."

"I'd rather you didn't," she said. "Anyone could be hiding in the trees."

"Let them hide." He fiddled with the combination of new locks she had installed. "I've changed my mind. I'm going rowing." His eyes darkened as he held her gaze. "There's more to this workaholic than you might think."

"Rick! Wait!" She grabbed her backpack from the couch and hurried across the room, reaching the door just as he unlocked the dead bolt. "Let me." His gaze froze on her lips before he stepped aside.

Unnerved by his nearness, she cracked open the door and peered outside. "You don't have to do this, Rick. It's not going to prove anything."

"I've got to do something," he said, his voice thin with impatience. "I can't sit around here all day twiddling my thumbs." He brushed past her and cleared the porch with hurried strides.

Locking the door behind her, she flew down the steps after him, scanning the woods as she hurried to keep up. As she ran, she slid the pack up her arm and over her shoulder.

The lake sparkled like a jewel beneath the bright morning sun, but it was no time to admire its beauty. Rick's safety was paramount in her mind.

Squinting against the glare, she pulled her sunglasses from a pocket of her backpack and slid them into place. "Stay on the trail," she cautioned, and his jaw tightened.

Once they reached the dock, she relaxed. The trees had thinned out, leaving fewer places for a gunman to hide.

Rick stepped into the rowboat and set to work scooping out the pine needles and cones.

"It doesn't look like it's been used for quite some time," she said. "What a pity."

"Yeah, well, my boss is almost as much of a workaholic as I am." Rick tossed the last of the dry needles out of the boat, wiped his hands on his jeans and held out his hand. "Watch your step."

Taking his outstretched hand, she stepped into the boat and sat facing the shore, her pack by her feet.

Sitting opposite her, he untied the bowline and

pushed the boat away from the dock. With a powerful hand on each oar he began rowing, the muscles of his sturdy arms rippling with each back and forth movement.

The gentle breeze ruffled his thick wavy hair, and the golden highlights matched the glints of sunlight reflecting off the water.

He looked up at her, and even though her eyes were hidden behind her sunglasses, she couldn't hide the fact that she was watching him.

Turning her head, she spotted a duck alongside the boat, followed by two downy ducklings. Jumping at the chance to draw his attention away from her, she pointed. "Oh, look. Aren't they adorable?"

His face broke into a wide smile. He no longer looked angry or out to prove something. He appeared to be a man having the time of his life. With the worry lines on his forehead all but gone for a change, he looked younger and relaxed.

By now they had traveled a safe distance from shore, and she decided to follow his example and relax.

Even a high-powered rifle couldn't reach them out this far. It was perfectly safe out here. Rick was safe. She was…okay, not safe, exactly, but as long as she stayed in her seat and Rick stayed in his, she had a shot at keeping her professional integrity.

It was a comforting thought as long as she didn't dwell on the fact that she and Rick appeared to be the only two people in the whole wide world. Or that the boat seemed even smaller now that they were in the middle of the lake. Smaller and more intimate.

Closing her eyes, she lifted her face to the sun, soaking up the warm rays. She needed this break almost as much as her client did. She sighed in relief. *Client, client, client.* There, she'd done it. She'd wiped everything out of her mind except for the fact that she was in a boat with her *client* and this was just part of the job.

If only she hadn't opened her eyes, she might have gone on believing such nonsense indefinitely. But once she made visual contact with him, her senses spun out of control.

This time it was Rick who was doing the staring. Only he made no attempt to hide it. His eyes lingered on her mouth, hungrily, creating a burning sensation that she couldn't control, even when she moistened her lips.

For several moments, they sat looking at each other. Rick's eyes never wavered from her face as he rowed the boat with smooth, powerful strokes.

Desperate to break the taut silence, she said the first thing that came to mind. "Now isn't this better than work?"

He gave her a lopsided grin. "You'll make a believer out of me yet."

She smiled back, but it wasn't easy. Smiling beneath his steady gaze was like trying to smile during a passionate kiss. "I'm…glad."

"Just don't tell my boss. When he sent me up here, I don't think this is what he had in mind."

"He sounds like a bulldog."

"A pit bull would be more like it."

"So why do you work for him?"

"Why?" Rick's eyes clung to hers. "It's a great company. They're on the cutting edge of technology, and they aren't afraid to let an employee run with an idea. What about you? Why are you working for the S. J. Spade *Insurance* Agency?"

"The owner, Samantha Spade, is my aunt."

He looked surprised. "Is that right?"

"Do you know her personally?"

"No, but my office manager does."

"That explains why you called her."

"Why wouldn't I? Your aunt's company is supposed to be the best in the Bay Area."

"It is. But male clients are few and far between. The last four digits of the telephone number actually translate into the word *hero*. Not too many men are brave enough to dial a number like 1-800-555-*HERO*."

He looked startled for a moment before throwing his head back and laughing out loud. "I don't believe it. No wonder Lorraine looked so secretive when I asked her to call for me." He regarded Jacquie thoughtfully. "I imagine a woman wishing to hire herself a hero might not be too happy when a lady bodyguard showed up."

"Some men aren't all that happy, either," she reminded him.

"All right, so I made a mistake. I just hope you're as hard on a potential killer as you are on me."

"You think you've seen me in action?" she asked. "I've got news for you. You haven't seen anything yet."

He lifted both oars out of the water. "Now that's something to think about." His eyes smoldered and the burning dark depths held the kind of promise that made even the most resistant part of her want to surrender.

She tore her gaze away from his and pretended to study the shoreline. In reality, her heart was racing so hard she couldn't concentrate on anything.

He resumed rowing. "According to Lorraine, your aunt is rather…formidable."

She chanced a glance at him. "The chief of police once said he'd rather face a prison riot than face my aunt's wrath."

"So why did you agree to work for her?"

"She's been like a second mother to me. She never had a daughter of her own. I think she always hoped that I would follow in her footsteps. I told her I'd give her a year."

"That's very generous of you. A year's a long time to put one's own plans on hold. Most people would have told her no."

"I couldn't…" Jacquie hesitated, afraid to tell him the real reason she'd agreed to work for her aunt, for fear he would laugh. But something about being in a boat alone with him lulled her into a sense of security. At that moment, she felt she could trust him explicitly. "When I was a child, my aunt Samantha was the one person in all the world who took the time to watch a sunset with me. That's why I couldn't say no."

He didn't laugh, but for several moments he rowed in silence, watching her as if she was a puzzle that only he could solve.

"Oh, look," she said, jumping at the chance to distract him. "There's a trout." She leaned over the side of the boat to take a closer look.

"Oh, no! It's caught on a fish hook." The fishing line was attached to a floating log a short distance away. She reached over the side of the boat and tried to grab hold of the nylon line.

"Careful," he cautioned. "Or you'll overturn the boat." He moved onto the seat next to her, making the boat level again by balancing her weight.

The line floated out of reach. "I need a net," she said. "Something…"

"Here." He unbuttoned his shirt and pulled it off. His magnificent chest glistened in the sunlight, and it was all she could do to keep from staring.

Taking the shirt in her hand, the warmth of his body still radiating from the knit fabric, she met his gaze briefly before turning away. She then lowered the shirt into the water and let it float beneath the fish. "I've got it!" she sang out.

"You're going to fall in," he cautioned. He grabbed hold of the waistband of her shorts and his fingers practically set her lower spine on fire.

Distracted momentarily by his touch, she almost let the fish get away. But she managed to undo the hook and lower the fish back into the water. The trout floated for a short time, then turned on its side.

"Oh, no." No sooner had she cried out in dismay, thinking the fish dead, than it suddenly swam away and disappeared into the depths of the lake. Feeling strangely giddy, she pulled back, laughing in delight. "We saved him."

Rick let go of her waistband, his fingers skimming her smooth flesh as he worked his arm around her torso. His velvety voice caressed her ear. "*You* saved him."

Momentarily forgetting to breathe, she gasped for air, but she was so frazzled, she inadvertently let go of his shirt. "Oh, no!" She tried to retrieve it, but he stopped her.

"It's all right," he assured her.

"But…" She turned to face him. Maybe it was all right for him, but one glimpse of his bare chest and her female senses took to spinning like a top.

Eyes dancing, he took her wet, cold hand in his and rubbed it until warmth was restored. Afraid to move for fear of breaking the magical spell that held her in its grip, she gazed up at him, mesmerized. How handsome he looked with the sun in his hair, on his face, warming his eyes, his mouth, his chest. How very, very sexy.

His gaze dropped to her lips, and she practically melted on the spot. "Jack…" he murmured.

That did it! It was time to put a stop to this. All she had to do was say the word, push him away, jump overboard. Indeed, she tried; she really did try. She pressed her hands flat against that dreamy chest of his, ready to do her basic man-overboard push. She would have succeeded, too. If only his honey-warm lips hadn't gotten in the way…

13

HIS LIPS FELT like heaven. And his hands on her back, in her hair, on her thigh—all over her—now that felt like heaven, too.

He circled her wrist with his fingers and gently pulled her away from the side of the boat. Cupping her face with his hands, he coaxed her to her knees.

"Aunt Samantha is going to…" The rest of her sentence was swallowed up by the sweet warm command of his lips.

His male fragrance filled her head. His warm, teasing kisses filled her soul. Running the palms of her hands up the sun-heated warmth of his magnificent bare chest, she wrapped her arms around his neck and opened her mouth to his probing tongue.

Oooh, her aunt would kill her. *Thou shalt not…*

No sooner did the thought occur to her than her mind went blank, or partially blank. All Jacquie could recall with any real clarity was something about a beautiful garden and the delectable taste of forbidden fruit.

She surrendered to the magical play of his hands on her body. The scope of his touch, the power of his kisses matched the rugged splendor of the mountains, which seemed to form a protective barrier around them.

Sighing in contentment, she pressed against him. He slid his hand beneath her knit shirt and cupped his fingers around a breast that literally ached for his touch. His lips lingered at the hollow at her neck. Bolts of electricity traveled down her spine, making her tingle with pleasure.

The earth actually moved, or that's what she thought at first. In reality, the boat was rocking like a cradle in a windstorm.

"Careful," he whispered. He eased his back against a pile of faded flotation cushions. He then pulled her on top of him and held her tightly against him, kissing her gently until the rocking had slowed to a gentle sway, and her body was ready to explode.

Straddling his legs with her own, her hands in the lush fullness of his hair, she showered his face with heated kisses, then settled her mouth against his.

He unzipped her shorts and ever so carefully drew them down her legs until she was able to kick them off. The next thing to go was her vest, followed by her shoulder holster and shirt and finally, her pretty lace bra.

He drew back slightly as if in awe and gazed at her full, rounded breasts. "You're even more beautiful than I imagined," he whispered. He touched both ivory mounds tenderly before cradling first one, then the other in his hand and teasing the rosy tips into little rosebuds.

She trailed her hands up and down his chest and back, breathing warm kisses along his warm neck. He drew an aching crest into his mouth and she interrupted her shower of kisses to let out a little cry of ecstasy.

"Hold on tight," he whispered.

Slowly, he rolled her onto her back, tucking a cushion beneath her head. The boat rocked frantically and little laps of water trickled over the side.

Once he was on top of her, he tucked her curves beneath him before lowering his body ever so gently onto hers. He then held her closely and waited for the boat to settle into a gentle roll before his mouth followed the smooth lines of her flesh all the way to her hips.

She pressed the lower half of her body against the hard, hot arousal centered between his own thrusting hips, and his body trembled in response.

He reached for his zipper. "Where's that damn survival kit of yours?" he rasped in her ear. "I feel a shark attack coming on."

"It's behind me," she said.

He reached over her head to grab her canvas pack, rocking the boat again. It took him only a moment to strip off his jeans and take care of business, but to her, it seemed like a long and torturous wait.

"Hurry!" she urged. Her heated body cried out for release.

He settled his hard naked body on top of hers and she squirmed beneath him, enjoying the feel of his manly shaft against her pelvis. He trailed his fingers down the length of her to the moist sweet softness between her thighs.

Shivers of delight, of pure ecstasy, of pure exquisite need, racked her; flames of desire engulfed her.

He entered her, filling her body, her very soul, with his incredible strength, and began to thrust powerfully.

She cried out and clung to him as a myriad of sensations exploded inside her. Even the dangerous movements of the boat couldn't compete with the quaking waves of ecstasy that washed over her.

He shuddered and cried out her name. Breathing hard, he clung to her, gasping for air. Neither moved until the boat stopped rocking and the world stopped spinning.

She blew against his heated chest, watching the golden, crisp hairs move beneath her breath. "My aunt's going to kill me."

"Your aunt won't know."

"You don't know my aunt," she said. "She'll know."

He trailed a finger down her nose to her lips, his eyes filled with softness. "Until this moment, I don't believe I knew anything about anything." He kissed her gently on the lips before pulling away. "The sun's hot on my back."

Taking in the magnificent splendor of his naked body, Jacquie felt a shivery response in her own. "We better get dressed before we both get sunburned."

His eyes lingered on her as if he wanted to capture the moment forever in his memory. "You're right," he drawled. "A full-body sunburn would surely make your aunt suspicious. I'll keep the boat balanced while you get dressed."

Her underwear, shorts and shirt were partly wet from the water at the bottom of the boat, but she quickly dressed, welcoming the coolness against her heated flesh.

After slipping her shoulder holster in place, she finger combed her hair and surveyed the shoreline. Even knowing there would be consequences to pay for what had occurred, nothing could spoil the feeling of contentment she felt.

She tensed, suddenly. A flash of light in the distance caught her eye. Squinting against the blinding sun that angled off some metal object, she grabbed her binoculars and scanned the shore.

A motorcycle was parked a short distance from the little dock. Lowering the glasses, she narrowed her eyes.

If that motorcycle belonged to the same man she had seen by the dock on her first day in Falcon Heights, and later in town, then Rick's stalker had returned.

She glanced at Rick. His smooth bare back was toward her as he strived to steer the boat away from the same log they had spotted earlier. Not wanting to alarm him, she decided to say nothing. At least for now. As long as they were this far out, there wasn't any way the stalker could harm them. Unless...

Suddenly she recalled one of the videos shown in bodyguard boot camp. The film showed how a terrorist had managed to kill his prey by attaching a bomb to the underside of a yacht.

What if the stalker had attached a bomb to the bottom of the rowboat? It was possible. And what if that same bomber was getting ready at that very moment to discharge it?

Convinced she was right, and without a moment to spare, she leaped toward Rick. Rick, who had not yet gotten around to dressing, was caught off balance. With a startled look, he fell overboard, taking her with him.

The water was icy cold. She came up sputtering, arms splashing wildly. Her panic subsided when she felt Rick's arms around her waist, but not her concern.

"Are you okay?" he yelled.

Her teeth chattering, she blinked the water out of her eyes and pulled away from him. "Get away from the boat!"

With frantic strokes, she swam toward shore, Rick hot on her heels. "Jack!" he called.

She was a strong swimmer, but the cold water bit into her flesh. By the time she reached the shallows, she was not only shivering, her lower limbs were practically numb.

She stood, the water up to her knees, her clothes clinging to her body, and scanned the shoreline. The dock was hidden behind the trees, so there was no way of knowing if the motorcycle was still parked there.

Rick's head popped up from the water, his face a mask of cold fury. "Are you out of your mind?" he shouted.

"Shhh." She listened, but all she could hear was the raucous cries of a distant scrub jay.

"What the hell is going on? I'm freezing my buns off and..." He stood and started toward shore.

"Wait!" She grabbed him by the arm. "I saw your stalker. I thought he placed a bomb in the boat."

"Trust me. There was no bomb anywhere near that boat." Rick waded away from her.

"Well, there could have been!" she called after him. She pulled her gun out of its holster and prayed the water hadn't harmed it. Damn fool. He could get himself shot!

Wading after him, she stepped on a jagged rock with a bare foot. "Ouch!" Her temper snapped and she raised her voice. "Would you please slow down?"

Ignoring her, he walked onto shore, his magnificent body glistening in the bright sunlight. Suddenly, the humor of the situation hit her and she giggled. She couldn't help it. Rick was buck naked.

Her laughter died as suddenly as it had begun. Concern for his safety took precedence the moment he disappeared among the thick growth.

Moving quickly, she raced up the slight incline of the stony bank. She would never forgive herself if anything happened to him. "Rick!"

She almost collapsed with relief when he stepped out from behind a bush. Her gaze dropped to the pine branch he held beneath his waist.

It wasn't exactly a fig leaf, but it served the same purpose. She tried to stifle her giggles, to no avail.

Rick glowered at her. "It's not nice to laugh at Mother Nature."

"I know," she said. "But I can't help it." She surveyed the area around the dock, but there was no sign of the motorcycle. She prayed the stalker had taken off. No doubt he had.

Still, she'd feel a whole lot better once Rick was safely back inside the cabin. Besides, her clothes were soaking wet and she was freezing. With her sandals no doubt at the bottom of the lake, it was hard to walk.

"Let's go back," she said, replacing her gun. "All I want is a nice hot bath and some hot soup." Studying Rick's bare buns, she added playfully, "And a camera."

He turned to face her. "I'll give you a camera!" He leaped toward her, but she dodged before he caught her. "Come here, you coward!"

He chased her around a tree, grabbing her arm and trapping her against a tree trunk. Talk about being caught between a rock and a hard…

He abandoned his mock fig leaf and pressed his aroused body to hers.

Her dripping wet form tingled with welcome warmth as hot blood began to race through her. He caught her face between his hands and kissed her. She melted against him, rivulets of water settling around her feet, and answered his lips with equal fervor.

He withdrew his mouth and feathered his lips up her neck, his teeth clicking against the gold stud in her ear.

Pressing her body to his, she suddenly froze, then pulled away.

"Something wrong?" he asked.

She reached for her gun and held a finger to her mouth. "I heard something," she whispered. It sounded like the rustle of bushes.

He ducked, grabbing his pine codpiece, and quickly covered himself. It wasn't easy. This time there was more of him to cover. "What did you hear?"

A branch snapped behind her. She spun around and aimed her gun. "Come out with your hands up."

A man stepped out of the bushes, his hands raised over his head. She recognized him immediately as the same man she'd spotted by the dock.

Rick moved to her side. "Don't I know you from somewhere?" He snapped his fingers, trying to recall the man's name.

"The name's Harrison. We met, remember? I'm an FBI agent. I have ID."

"Let's see it," Jacquie said, keeping her gun aimed directly at him. "And take it nice and easy."

The man slid a hand into the pocket of his leather jacket and held up his badge.

"Now I remember," Rick said. "The day of the

bombing. You were the agent who questioned me."

Jacquie lowered her gun. "So what are you doing here?"

"Someone sent a bomb through the U.S. mails. That's a federal offense. I've been assigned to the case." He looked Rick up and down and cleared his throat. Apparently, it wasn't often that he came across a naked man in the line of duty. "Uh…someone tried to kill you once. Chances are that same someone will try again."

Jacquie's temper flared. "Rick should have been told that the FBI were having him followed. As his bodyguard, *I* should have been told."

"Sorry, ma'am, I'm only doing my job."

"And that's what I'm trying to do," Jacquie retorted. She took a deep breath. This was no time to argue over procedure. Besides, she was grateful the FBI was taking the bomb seriously. Rick sure wasn't. "Any suspects?"

The agent stared at her through his sunglasses. "Just one."

Now they were getting somewhere. She tucked her gun back into its holster. "So who is it? Who's trying to kill Rick?"

A granite-hard expression crossed the agent's face. "You are, ma'am. You're our only suspect."

14

"OF ALL THE RIDICULOUS, asinine things I've ever heard, this takes the cake!" Jacquie had been accused of a lot of things in her life, most of it deserved, but never had she been accused of trying to *kill* someone. At least not on purpose. "Did you hear what he said? I'm a suspect!"

Rick groaned with exasperation. "For the hundredth time, I heard. Remember? I was there."

She swung around to face him. "How dare he suggest I tried to kill you."

Fresh from his shower, Rick was dressed in a terry-cloth robe that failed to reach his knees and barely covered his chest. He leaned against the doorjamb of the kitchen, his arms crossed in front of him. "I don't know why you're so riled up. You can hardly blame Harrison for jumping to that particular conclusion. You *did* nearly kill me. Three times, that I can think of."

She stopped pacing. He was enjoying this; she was convinced of it. "They were accidents. Besides, what would be my motivation? Until three days ago, I never set eyes on you."

"Aren't you the one who said a murderer didn't need a motive?"

She looked at him incredulously. "Don't tell me you think I'm a suspect, too?"

"Of course not. I'm simply pointing out that Harrison has good reason to be suspicious."

"Maybe before," she conceded. "But I explained why I pushed you out of the boat."

"And you did a commendable job placing the full blame on Harrison's shoulders."

"Yeah, well...it *was* his fault. Just as it was his fault I pushed you in front of that car."

"You made that clear, too. So you see? You have nothing to worry about. You're not a suspect, Harrison is! Besides, if you ever do succeed in killing me, I know it would not be intentional."

She rolled her eyes. "And it was damn thoughtful of you to say as much to Harrison."

Rick's eyes sparkled with warm humor. "You didn't think I'd let him throw out all those accusations without standing up for you, did you? I'll tell you what. I'll make you some hot soup. That should calm you down."

"I don't want any soup. Besides, how can I calm down? I didn't even know that Harrison *was* a federal agent. I thought he was the man who was trying to kill you."

"You weren't supposed to know his identity. He's working undercover."

"I've been trained to sniff those guys out a mile away. That's my job. What kind of a bodyguard am I when I can't even tell the good guys from the bad?"

"Come on, Jack. Don't be so hard on yourself. You've been somewhat distracted lately." Rick tilted her chin upward and kissed the tip of her nose before heading for the kitchen.

She grabbed the back of a chair and closed her eyes. She'd been distracted, all right. Too gosh darn distracted, and she had no excuse for her unprofessional behavior. By allowing herself to get involved with Rick, she had jeopardized his safety, and that was reprehensible.

Getting herself pegged as a suspect in a federal investigation only added to her misery. Once Samantha got wind that her niece was a suspect there was no telling what she would do.

In the course of three days, Jacquie had managed to break at least half of the commandments according to Samantha Spade. Now she was about to break yet another one. Her job was to protect her client, not track down the culprit. But hell, someone had to do it, and if she was the best suspect the FBI could dig up, then that someone had better be her.

She opened her eyes and took a deep breath before moving to the kitchen. "Rick, the FBI is taking the bomb seriously, and I think you should, too. I want to go over that list of acquaintances with you again. I'm convinced someone wants to see you dead."

Rick dumped a can of soup into a pot. "You're barking up the wrong tree, Jack. Like I told Harrison, I don't have any enemies."

"None that you know of," she corrected.

"All right, if you insist." He glanced at his watch. "As soon as we eat, we better head for town. The UPS is due at four and my computer better be on that truck."

"All right," Jacquie said. "You drive and I'll take notes."

He frowned. "Notes."

"Yeah. We're going to catch ourselves a bomber or my name's not Jack."

LATER THAT NIGHT, Rick worked on his new computer, stopping only long enough to wolf down the dinner Jacquie prepared for him. She'd even made a chocolate soufflé. It was the least she could do to make up for all the trouble she'd caused.

While he worked, Jacquie sat on the couch cross-legged and studied the list of names. They were mostly Rick's co-workers and business associates. As far as she could tell, Rick's social life was totally nonexistent and had been for quite some time.

Rather than feeling relief, she felt depressed, for it only proved what she suspected was true: Rick could make her heart beat like no other man she'd ever met, but there was no future with him.

He was good for a roll in the hay—or a rowboat—but he was a workaholic, and she knew from bitter experience what it was like to love someone whose only priority in life was work.

As much as she loved her parents and admired their many accomplishments, she could never forget how abandoned she'd felt as a child.

She also knew her parents would have been shocked had she told them how she felt. They loved her, of course, but there was just so much time in any given day, so much energy to spare, and both poured everything they had into their careers.

Not once had her father made it to any of her softball games. He hadn't even made it to the school play the year she'd landed a leading role. Okay, so she'd played the part of the lonely little petunia in the onion patch, a role that seemed to parallel her own life. And yes, they probably would have been there had her mother not been on a book tour and her father not been testifying in front of a senate hearing. But try telling that to an eight-year-old kid who had just landed a part in the school play.

As the oldest child, she had been at the bottom of the totem pole in terms of family priority. It no longer angered her, not like it used to. But there was no way in hell she would consider spending her adulthood fighting for a man's attention.

Not that she was all that anxious to resume her role as the lonely little petunia. But what choice did she have?

What had happened between her and Rick could never be repeated. She swallowed the lump that rose in her throat and resisted the urge to wallow in self-pity.

She had only herself to blame. By allowing her heart to rule, she'd let her aunt down, put Rick's life in jeopardy and somehow managed to make herself more miserable than she'd ever felt in her life.

What if the bomber really *had* planted a bomb beneath the boat? Rick could have been killed, and all because she had failed to do the job she'd been sent to do.

What if Harrison had turned out to be the bomber instead of an FBI agent? What chance would Rick have had then? Standing in the woods, unarmed, naked as the day he was born. Gloriously nude. Gloriously aroused. Gloriously…

Heavenly days. There I go again. Thinking things I have no business thinking about.

If anything happened to Rick, she would never forgive herself. From this moment on, her every thought, her every action must be directed toward one thing and one thing alone: assuring Rick's complete safety.

Her gaze traveled over to the desk where he sat deep in thought. For once, he wasn't glowering at the monitor, but lines of concentration were visible on his face. It probably wasn't the time to recite the client-bodyguard commandments to him.

She went back to her notes and the list of names she had read through so many times she practically had them memorized. Who wanted to see Rick dead? His boss? Lorraine, his sixty-something office manager? His best friend, Lenny? His apartment manager? The girl he'd broken up with three years ago? Maybe Rick was right. Maybe it had been some disgruntled employee.

Around eleven o'clock that night, Rick let out a loud whoop. Had she not been half-asleep, Jacquie might not have nearly jumped out of her skin.

"That's it!" He leaped out of his chair and

bounced around the room like a rubber ball. "That's it."

"What?" She sat up and placed her hand on her chest to calm her racing heart. "You nearly scared me to death. What's it?"

"The problem that's been plaguing me all these weeks. I solved it!" He grabbed her hand and pulled her to her feet. "You were right! A day off did me wonders." With an arm around her waist, he lifted her off the floor and twirled her in a circle.

Laughing, she begged him to put her down. He lowered her until her toes touched the floor, but he didn't let her go. Instead, he held her close, his body pressing into hers. "You are a genius."

With his eyes soft as candlelight, he gazed down at her. *Thou shalt not fraternize with clients*, she repeated to herself. But come to think of it, fraternizing was the last thing on her mind. To prove it, she leaned against him and lifted her head. At that moment, she would have followed him to the moon.

His lips practically absorbed hers before searing a fiery path down her neck, where he nipped her skin playfully.

His hands explored her back, his sinewy fingers playing a full orchestra piece along her tingling spine. He then cupped his hands around her buttocks and pressed her to his pelvis, molding her every womanly curve against his hard lean form.

They had been forced to control their movements in the rowboat, but there was nothing to limit them now. A stack of books went flying as he pulled off his bathrobe. She accidentally overturned a chair as she kicked off her sweatpants. Backing her against a wall, he knocked a framed picture to the floor in his haste to pull off her knit top.

Lifting her in his arms, he carried her through the open door of his bedroom and stopped in his tracks. "Welcome to the *loving* zone," he said in teasing reference to her constant warnings about the killing zone.

"I don't think I've ever been in a loving zone before," she murmured softly in his ear.

He lowered her gently, lovingly onto the rumpled bed. Covering her body with his own naked form, he pressed his hand against her breast before lowering the strap of her bra to reveal an ivory mound. "What you do to me, Jack."

Since her professional name only reminded her of her aunt's rules of conduct, she whispered back, "The name's Jacquie."

"Jacquie, huh?" he whispered. "I like that even better."

They made wonderful and passionate love for the remainder of the night. They made glorious love, taking only the shortest possible time to catch their breath before starting all over again.

Rick threw himself into lovemaking as he threw himself into his work.

With single-minded purpose, he aroused the most fantastic sensations. He made love to her countless times and in countless ways, making each experience new and exciting. One time they made love fast and furiously, then later, they discovered each other all over again in a slow and gentle way.

When at last she thought she had nothing more to give, he coaxed her into making love in a way that was even more hot and steamy than before.

At one point, Jacquie felt so completely sated, so deliciously satisfied, she didn't think she could move. She lay in his arms and drifted into a sweet and blissful sleep, her body molding against his like a piece from the same jigsaw puzzle.

She awoke to find Rick devouring every inch of her body with his heated lips and fiery tongue, teasing her until fresh waves of desire washed over her. That's when he took her in what could only be described as the death-at-dawn type of lovemaking that most people could only dream about.

That did it. After that fine performance, even Rick was unable to do anything but lie back and gasp for air.

Smiling to herself, she laid her hand on the now soft manly organ that had brought her such pleasure, and fell into a deep and dreamless sleep.

15

THE NEXT MORNING, Rick rolled over. Even before he opened his eyes or gained full consciousness, he reached for her. It was a newly learned habit and one he intended to pursue from this day forward.

Finding the bed empty, he snapped open his eyes and bolted upward. "Jacquie!"

She was gone. Gone not just from his bed, but from the cabin. He felt it, sensed it. The house had a hollow ring to it, as if someone had emptied it of all its furnishings.

Jumping out of bed, he stormed to the window, yanking open the draperies, mindless of the dangers. Though the sun streamed through the glass to the walls and floor, not a flicker of light seemed to penetrate the gloom that filled the room now that she was gone.

Grabbing his robe, he ran naked through the house, pushing his arms into the sleeves as he went.

One glance out the front window confirmed his suspicions. Her car was gone, but Agent Harrison was standing guard, wearing a dark suit and tie.

Rick didn't have to go upstairs to know that her clothes would be gone, too.

He turned, spotting a note propped up against his computer, and his blood turned cold.

He fingered the note before unfolding it, dreading what awaited him. "Dear Rick," he read. "A bodyguard must put the life of a client above all other considerations. I'm afraid I've not done that. What happened between us was a terrible mistake and it will never happen again. Agent Harrison agreed to stand guard until your new bodyguard arrives."

It was signed "Jack."

He rolled the letter into a ball and tossed it into the wastebasket. What did she mean, it was a terrible mistake? How could what they shared be a mistake, terrible or otherwise?

It hurt that she had so little regard for him, for the memorable night they'd shared together. He couldn't believe it! She'd walked away as if he meant nothing to her, as if what happened was no more important to her than a one-night stand.

She didn't even care enough to tell him to his face that she was leaving. Well, if that's how she felt, he'd be damned if he would chase after her!

He had work to do.

It was less than three weeks before production was scheduled to begin. He couldn't afford to lose another hour, let alone toss away another full day. It would take at least five, maybe six hours to drive to San Francisco. Then he would have to track her down. He didn't even know where she lived. He knew nothing about her.

He knew everything.

He knew how she liked to be held and where

she liked to be touched. He knew every nuance of her body, of her voice, and how her eyes shimmered with afterglow. He had learned to read even the faintest subtleties of her smile. Never had he felt so close to another human being. He ached with the knowledge that having at last found his soul mate—his *life* mate—he might have already lost her.

If he thought he had half a chance, a fraction of a chance, he might be tempted to chase her down. What was he saying? He *was* tempted.

He glanced at his watch before catching himself. He had no intention of driving to San Francisco. Certainly not to track down a know-it-all woman who was as dangerous to his heart as she was to his bodily welfare.

He plopped himself down in front of his laptop and frantically began to click the mouse, darting in and out of files aimlessly. *Damn woman!* Click, click. *Who does she think she is?* Click, click. *How could she do this to me?*

Someone tapped at the door. *Aha! So she's come to her senses, has she?* Well, he would let her beg a little before hauling her into the loving zone and making her regret she'd ever put him through this hell.

He raced across the room and practically ripped the door off its hinges. "It's about—"

It wasn't Jack. It was the damn FBI agent standing next to what surely must be the tallest man in the world.

"Sorry to bother you," Harrison said, though he

didn't look the least bit sorry. "This is your new bodyguard."

Rick stared at three hundred pounds of pure muscle.

"The name's Tim," the man said, without a hint of humor.

"I'm sure you'll be in good hands," Harrison said.

Rick was about to tell Tiny Tim that he didn't need a bodyguard, but the grim-faced giant didn't look about to take any guff from him.

"If you need me, I'll be out front," Tim said.

"Thanks," Rick muttered. He would bet the guy had never been fired in his life. Rick slammed the door shut and went back to his desk. But it was impossible to concentrate on work.

He couldn't stop thinking about Jacquie. About how she felt in his arms. How the taste of her luscious warm body still lingered on his lips. How the delicate fresh fragrance of her seemed to permeate his skin, stamping him with a scent that titillated, even as it tortured him.

Adding to his misery, or at least his lack of concentration, was Tiny Tim. The bodyguard paced back and forth on the front porch, his heavy footsteps shaking the cabin walls until an oil painting crashed to the floor. An entire army marching across the porch couldn't have made more noise.

"That does it!" Rick stormed across the room and yanked open the door.

Tiny Tim turned and faced him, the scowl on his face indicating his annoyance. "I'd rather you didn't stand there. The front door is a security risk—"

"I know all about the killing zone," Rick said irritably. "I just want to tell you that I've changed my mind. I don't need a bodyguard. You can go. You're fired." He slammed the door shut, and when Tiny Tim didn't come bursting through it in a fit of rage, he heaved a sigh. Now maybe he could get some work done.

He sat in front of his computer and rubbed his hands together. Nothing, but nothing was going to interfere with his work now. Not Tiny, not Jack. Nothing.

Only it wasn't Jack that seemed to stare back from his monitor. It was Jacquie. Or rather it was her big blue eyes. Rick blinked and pounded the keys of his keyboard. It worked. No longer did he imagine seeing her eyes. Now it was the vision of her naked body that taunted him.

Things got worse as the morning progressed, or rather, his imagination grew more vivid. Twice he thought he'd heard her laugh.

By ten o'clock, he gave up and turned off his laptop. He was not going to get any work accomplished, no matter how hard he tried.

After cooking an omelette that he had no desire to eat, he decided there was only one way to handle this. He grabbed his denim jacket off the wooden hook in the living room and flung it over his shoulder.

He cracked open the door and peered outside in a way that was sure to please even the most obsessive bodyguard. Not only was he acting like a lovesick adolescent, he had turned into a paranoid nutcase. It was not a good sign.

After he was certain all was quiet on the western front, he hurried to his car. He put the Blazer into four-wheel-drive and sped away, leaving a cloud of dust in his wake.

He should reach San Francisco by six that afternoon. With a little luck, he'd catch Jacquie at the office—assuming, of course, she had gone to the office—and have it out with her.

So it was over, was it? So she didn't have any feelings for him? Well, let her tell him that to his face!

16

JACQUIE'S APARTMENT was on the third floor of a brick building that had twice escaped condemnation by the city. Supposedly, the building had historical significance, though no one could agree exactly what that significance was.

Jacquie had opted for the third floor because she wanted a balcony. But any asset she gained was negated by the temperamental elevator. It wasn't the first time the elevator had become stuck between floors.

Muttering to herself, she hauled her belongings up the three flights of stairs. She let herself into her apartment, leaving her duffel bag and boxes in the entryway.

She blinked hard, trying to erase Rick's face from her thoughts. He'd never stepped foot in her apartment, but everything seemed to remind her of him.

She'd driven straight home from Falcon Heights, stopping only twice. Once for gas and another time to wipe the tears from her eyes and clear her vision. She was tired, exhausted. No wonder she was imagining things.

She went through her mail, watered her plants and tried to get up the nerve to face her aunt.

Samantha would never call her at home on

business. It wasn't her style. Her aunt always did things if not in a professional way, at least in a dramatic way. She'd wait until Jacquie was in the office before letting her have it.

Jacquie's spirits lifted momentarily; if she never went to the office, she wouldn't have to explain what had happened in Falcon Heights—not ever.

"Chicken," she muttered. *Since when have you been afraid to face Aunt Samantha?* Besides, she hadn't really done anything wrong. Immoral, maybe.

But not wrong.

All right, that did it! She would go to the office that very afternoon and face her aunt. Jacquie might have been a chicken at times in her past, but she was not about to act like one now!

It was late, after five, before she walked up the steps of the stately Victorian house that served as headquarters for her aunt's protective-service agency. Jacquie paused in front of the stained-glass front doors and tried to brace herself before letting herself inside.

She had taken the precaution of dressing up for the occasion. Her aunt wasn't opposed to those around her begging for forgiveness as long as they did so in style.

Dressed in a teal-colored suit, a scarf tied cheekily around her neck and high heels, Jacquie crossed the parquet floor of the reception area.

Charilyn looked up from her desk, the phone at her ear. Upon seeing Jacquie, her smooth dark skin crinkled with worry lines. Not a good sign.

Telling herself there were worse fates than facing the wrath of her aunt—and one day she might even think of one—Jacquie walked through the frosted-glass-paneled doors and up the winding staircase to the second floor.

She passed the other offices, most of them empty. The other agents were either on assignment or had gone home for the day.

She threw open the door at the end of the hall. It didn't seem possible, but her office appeared to have shrunk in size in the short time she had been in Falcon Heights.

Mark, who followed her into the office a few moments later, clucked his tongue and assured her the room wasn't any smaller, it only looked that way.

"Mr. Euclid replenished his cleaning supplies," Mark explained, pushing a cardboard box of paper towels against the wall.

Jacquie studied the rows of brass polish and other cleaners lined up like soldiers on both sides of her. There simply was no place left to store her tote bag.

"Did you find out anything from the police about the Westley case?"

Mark shook his head. "Only that there are no suspects. But you still owe me your recipe."

The phone rang and Jacquie eyed it nervously. "Don't tell me."

Looking apologetic, he shrugged as if to say things were out of his control. "I'm required to report everything to your aunt. I called her immediately, as soon as I spotted your car in front."

Jacquie took a deep breath and grabbed the phone just before the third ring.

"What happened this time?" Aunt Samantha demanded in her ear.

Holding up his crossed fingers, Mark left the office, closing the door quietly behind him.

"I…uh…Mr. Westley wasn't that gung ho on having a woman bodyguard."

"That's no reason to sleep with him."

She'd known she could never keep such a thing secret from her aunt, at least not for long. Her aunt had a sixth sense about such things. Still, Jacquie had never dreamed her secret would be out so soon.

"What makes you think I…?" she croaked. *Other than the fact that I sound like I'm choking to death.*

"I know you, and when you're trying to sound all businesslike with me, I know you're hiding something."

Jacquie took a deep breath. "I feel terrible, Aunt Samantha. First Lord Byron and now this. Maybe it would be better if I just turned in my resignation."

"A resignation is out of the question. No one resigns from my company. Not until I fire them. It's the only way. Besides, Lord Byron wasn't your fault."

"Even so…"

"As for Mr. Westley…now you know why I insist that my employees follow my commandments. As I'm sure you must recall, commandment number 311 clearly states—"

"I know, I know. 'Thou shalt never mix business with pleasure.' I'm really sorry, Aunt Samantha. I blew it."

"It's bad enough that you slept with him, you don't have to go into details."

"But I—"

"By God, you young'uns act like those of us who've been around for a year or two don't know anything. Why do you suppose I wrote all those commandments?"

Thinking she heard just a note of regret in her aunt's voice, Jacquie sat forward. Aunt Samantha seldom if ever discussed her private life, or her two—or was it three?—divorces. She also never spoke of her youth, because of some great tragedy that had supposedly happened way back when.

No one dared talk about it, and Jacquie just naturally assumed her aunt had suffered some great lost love. But she never really knew and the temptation to delve into her aunt's secret past was more than she could resist.

"Has it happened to you? Have you ever met a man who made you feel so utterly, utterly alive that you were willing to risk everything to be in his arms?"

"For heaven's sakes, Precious. Of course I have. Many times. You young people think you invented love."

Jacquie's jaw dropped. "I—I don't *love* him," she stammered. "I—I hardly know him. I mean, I only met him a few days ago. Not even a week and…"

"It was love at first sight. That's the best kind."

"No! It was not!" Attraction at first sight, maybe. Lust. But definitely *not* love!

"I hope what you say is true. I've got a business to run. It's bad enough that an agent of mine slept with a client. But to fall in love with one…now that would be a real problem. As a bodyguard, your duty is to put your life on the line for a client."

"I know—"

"A bodyguard mustn't hesitate to deflect a bullet."

"I would do anything to save Rick's life."

"I'm not talking about Rick. I'm talking about other clients. If you're in love with Rick, you're not going to risk your life to save another client, and that's a liability." She repeated almost verbatim a line from a speech she'd given at bodyguard boot camp. "It's a bodyguard's responsibility to remain agile, alert and emotionally unattached."

"You have nothing to worry about, Aunt Samantha. I told you. I'm not in love."

Her aunt didn't sound the least bit convinced. "Go home, clear your head, and if you still believe you have no feelings for Rick Westley this time next week, I'll assign you to another case. One that involves no animals and no men. Meanwhile, stay out of trouble."

The line went dead and Jacquie hung up, feeling more depressed than ever.

Now she'd done it. She'd let her aunt down. Lied to her. Actually, she hadn't lied. Not really. She'd said she wasn't in love with Rick and that was true. They'd had great sex together—the most wonderful sex she'd ever experienced—but that was all it was. Just sex.

Love didn't enter the picture. How could it? Rick was no doubt working away at his computer at that very moment. If the truth were known, he was probably relieved that she was no longer around to distract him—if he so much as noticed she was gone.

He would notice. Of course he would notice. Wouldn't he?

Oh, no, you don't! She'd cried most of the way to San Francisco. Shedding so much as another tear on Rick's behalf was out of the question.

All at once the walls felt like they were closing in on her. For a confused moment in time, she imagined an army of brass-polish cans circling her, about to take her hostage.

Grabbing her tote bag, she shot out of her office and headed down the hall.

She started down the stairs and froze, unable to believe her eyes. For heading up the stairs toward her was the last person she expected to bump into at her aunt's place of business. "Rick!" Heavenly days, he *had* noticed she was gone.

He raised his head and the look on his face was of pure relief. "Jacquie! Thank God you're still here." He bounded up the remaining stairs and pulled her away from the landing. "Is there a place we can talk?"

"I have nothing to say to you."

"Good. Then you won't interrupt me while I'm talking." He hustled her through the first open door and into an empty office. It was one of the choice offices that provided a sweeping view of the Golden Gate Bridge.

He released her and slammed the door shut behind them. "Jacquie—"

"The name's Jack," she said, glaring at him. She would never be Jacquie to him again!

"I want you to come back to Falcon Heights."

She gazed at him in astonishment. "You drove all the way here to tell me that? You lost a whole day of work to tell me you want me back?"

He frowned. "Don't remind me. I'll have to work night and day to make up the time."

She felt a sinking feeling inside. She should have known. "What a pity."

"So what do you say? Are you coming back or aren't you?"

No "please," no "I miss you," no nothing. She felt a stabbing pain inside. "You don't need me. My aunt's assigned another bodyguard to you."

"Who needs him? He's six foot ten and three hundred pounds of muscle."

"If I recall, that's exactly the kind of bodyguard you wanted."

"Well, now I want you."

"I don't want to be your bodyguard, Rick." Come to think of it, she didn't want to be anyone's bodyguard. "I'm a terrible bodyguard." It was hard to admit to yet another failure, but it was true.

Jack leaned against the desk and crossed his arms. "I wouldn't say that."

"I almost killed you twice."

"Uh...I think that was three times."

"See what I mean?"

"Maybe you are a bit overenthusiastic. But that's what I love about you."

"Love?" she whispered. "You *love* that I nearly killed you?"

"I love that you put your whole heart and soul into everything you do." He beseeched her with a lingering look. "Come back with me. Please, Jack, say you will."

"I can't, Rick." It took a great deal of effort to deny him his request, but she really had no choice. "I put your life in jeopardy by getting personally involved with you. On the boat..." Nearly overwhelmed by the warm memories of that day, she was forced to avert her eyes before she could finish what she had to say. "You could have been killed and it would have been all my fault."

"No, Jack, it wasn't your fault. I wanted you and I would have done anything to have you that day."

She lifted her eyes to him, clinging to his every word. God help her, she was tempted, so very, very tempted to take whatever little of himself he could offer her and forget the rest. But she couldn't.

For the first time in her life she had found something that really meant the world to her, and she wasn't willing to settle for less than the whole. If she couldn't have him on her terms, she couldn't have him at all.

"I wanted you, too," she admitted. "More than I've ever wanted anyone in my life."

A look of rapture crossed his face and he reached for her, but she quickly backed away.

"But don't you see? By giving in to my feelings, I let down you, my aunt, everyone. I even let myself down."

His brows drew together. "Maybe you're right. Maybe it's not a good idea for you to work for me. But you and I...we're good together. Last night was the most special night of my life." His voice grew hoarse, his eyes brimming with tenderness. "I'll never forget the night we shared for as long as I live."

"Last night..." Feeling her resolve begin to desert her, she crossed her arms in front of her and began again. "Last night was a mistake. It should never have happened."

"But it did."

"I want...oh, never mind."

"Tell me, Jack." He touched her arm beseechingly. "What do you want?"

"I want to be the most important person in someone's life." There, now she'd said it, said the very thing she didn't want to say because it sounded so self-centered and childish, maybe even selfish.

Regardless of how it sounded, it was the truth, and she was tired of pretending that her own needs and feelings didn't count. She was even more tired of living her life to please everyone else. She had studied law and business, even cooking, to please her father, and she had failed miserably. It was time she started living her life to please herself.

"Does that mean what I think it means?" he asked softly. "Do you want to be important to me? Because I sure as hell want to be important to you."

Her breath caught in her chest. "Don't," she whispered. "Don't say things that you think I want to hear."

He moved closer and lifted his hand to her cheek, pressing his palm to her flesh. Without meaning to, she pressed back. "When I woke and found you gone, I went crazy. I couldn't work. I couldn't do anything. All I could think about was you."

The tenderness in his eyes, in his voice, in his touch made her want to believe that anything was possible and that Rick really was capable of changing. "It was the same with me," she whispered, her vision blurred with tears. "I cried all the way to San Francisco."

"I almost ran out of gas because I didn't want to waste time stopping."

She gazed up at him, and the tears she'd stopped fighting now rolled down her cheeks unchecked. "I've never felt more miserable in my life."

"I've never felt so alone. Oh, Jack."

"Jacquie," she whispered.

"Jacquie." Her name fell from his lips in a silky whisper. He wiped her tears away with his thumbs. "Just as soon as I finish this project, we can...I have another project in the wings, but after I'm finished with that, I should be able to—"

He couldn't have hurt her more had he stabbed her. She pounded his chest with her fists. "Ohhh!"

He grabbed her by the wrists. "Jacquie?" He looked genuinely perplexed. "What is it?"

"Jack. The name's Jack." She pulled away from him. "And it's your work. It's always your work."

"That's not true—"

"Yes, it is."

Anger flashed in his eyes. "Aren't you being a bit unreasonable?"

Maybe so, but she didn't care. She forced herself to calm down. She'd never gotten around to telling her parents how their dedication to their work had affected her, but it was vital not to hold anything back from Rick.

"I like that your work's important to you, Rick. That's how it should be. But I don't like that it's the top priority in your life. You said it yourself— you don't even have time to see your own family. The people you care about."

He raked his fingers through his hair. "All right, I admit it. I've always been a workaholic. But I want to change."

"What if you can't?"

"We'll cross that bridge when we get to it."

She swallowed hard. "I can't take that chance."

He stepped toward her. "Isn't that what all couples must do? Take a chance on each other? Isn't that what love is all about?"

There it was again, the word *love*. The very thought that she might love him scared the hell out of her. But a part of her wanted it to be true, no matter how much it hurt. "I'm sorry, Rick. It's over between us. I think you better leave."

He opened his mouth to say something, but she waved her hand to stop him. "Go!" she pleaded. "Just go."

Cold fury masked his face. Without another word, he spun on his heel and left the office. The slamming of the door was a final blow to her already shattered heart.

She stood rigidly, her hands balled at her sides. She didn't move until the sound of his footsteps faded away.

17

RICK WAS GONE. It wasn't what she wanted, by any means, but it was the way things had to be. Hell, it hurt, hurt so much she could hardly stand it. It was all she could do to drag herself to the window for one last look at him, for one last goodbye.

The moment Rick walked into view on the sidewalk below, the pain inside her grew so intense she could hardly catch her breath. Blinking back tears, she touched the glass and followed his movements with her fingers.

Rick stepped off the curb, turning his head to check for traffic. All that was visible was his profile, but he looked angry and hurt, so unlike himself.

She ached, literally ached, for one of his sexy, teasing smiles. What she would give to see him look at her once more as he had last night—as he had a few moments ago.

Depressed, she rested her forehead against the cool windowpane and whispered his name. "Take care of yourself. Take *good* care of yourself."

She was desperate, suddenly, to talk to someone, anyone. No, not just anyone. She picked up the phone and dialed the number of her father's law firm. His office manager, Janet Wendell, answered.

"This is Jacquie. Is my father there? I need to talk to him. It's very important."

"Oh, hi, Jacquie. It's been a while. Hold on."

Pressing the receiver to her ear, she watched Rick dart across the street and slide behind the wheel of his Blazer.

Janet's voice floated across the line. "I'm sorry, Jacquie. Your father's in a meeting. If you call back in an hour or so, maybe he'll have time to talk to you then."

"Sure he will." Jacquie replaced the receiver.

Her feet were still rooted to the spot in front of the window, because she didn't want to let Rick out of her sight.

Suddenly, something occurred to her. She scanned the sidewalks, the street, the park across the street. Where was Tiny Tim? And why wasn't he doing the job he'd been assigned to do?

Rick drove away and still there was no sign of Tim. But she did notice a tan-colored van pull away from the curb seconds after Rick did, and she tensed.

It could be coincidental, of course, that another car had pulled away so soon, but she couldn't afford to take the chance. She pressed her forehead against the window and tried to read the license plate, but it was covered in mud. That did it. It hadn't rained in weeks.

She grabbed her tote bag and ran out of the office and down the stairs. She was parked in front, but it was necessary to hang an illegal U before she was heading in the right direction.

Driving faster than the speed limit, she darted

in and out of traffic. There was no sign of Rick's car or even the van. Knowing Rick, he was probably heading back to Falcon Heights to finish his project. In that case, he would be heading east on U.S. 101.

She pulled out her cellular phone with one hand and pushed a preset button. Mark answered on the first ring.

"Have you heard from Tiny Tim?" Jacquie asked.

"Yes, why?"

"He's not with Rick Westley."

"That's because Mr. Westley fired him. Said he didn't need a bodyguard."

She should have known. "Mr. Westley doesn't know what he's talking about." She pressed the End button and tossed the phone onto the seat.

Honking at the car in front, she eased onto the 101 and relaxed. Not two cars ahead was Rick's Blazer. For once the red color was an advantage, for it made it easy to pick him out. Of course, if she could spot him so easily, so could everyone else. She glanced in the rearview mirror and checked the lanes on either side. No sign of the van.

Keeping Rick in sight, she stayed two or three cars behind and followed him onto the I-80.

Traffic came to a full stop and she quickly pulled off her heels and changed into sandals. A van identical to the one she'd seen earlier passed her, two lanes over.

A van parked opposite her aunt's place of business, leaving almost the same time as Rick and winding up on the same freeway, could be mere coincidence, but somehow she doubted it.

She was almost positive someone was following Rick, and the very thought made her blood turn cold. She honked her horn, but it was a wasted effort. No one was moving and that meant Rick.

She told herself that nothing would happen on a busy freeway. The stalker would probably follow him back to Falcon Heights. In which case, she had time. She could easily catch up to Rick once they had left the city behind and hit the open road.

Taking advantage of the stopped traffic, she reached into her tote for change to pay for tolls and dug Harrison's business card out of her wallet. She tried both numbers listed on the fed's card, but either his phone was turned off or he was out of range.

She tossed the phone aside again and stared at the sea of taillights ahead. It was going to be a long haul back to Falcon Heights.

THREE AND A HALF of the most nerve-racking hours of her life crawled by during which she tried to stay close to Rick without his spotting her.

Presently, they were heading north on the I-5. The needle on her gas gauge was close to empty.

Suddenly, Rick's right turn signal began to blink.

Puzzled, she lifted her foot off the gas pedal. There was no sign of a service station or any other place of business that could possibly explain why Rick had pulled onto the shoulder of the roadway.

Something had to be wrong. She drove past him

and pulled into the driveway of a cement company a short distance ahead.

She parked and ran back, gun in hand, hiding behind a thick growth of oleander bushes growing on the side of the road.

Spotting Rick's car, she peered through the branches. He sat behind the wheel, staring at the road ahead, an odd, faraway look on his face.

Puzzled, she holstered her gun. What in the world was he doing? Did he have engine trouble? Was he out of gas? Had he spotted her car? What?

She paced in a circle, trying to decide what to do. She couldn't leave him stranded on the road. As far as she knew, they were miles away from the nearest gas station.

The last strains of a brilliant sunset were beginning to fade and it would soon be dark. Already, the first star of the night had made its appearance directly overhead.

Cars and diesel trucks sped by, but so far, the van was nowhere to be seen. She could call for help, of course—call the auto club, using her own card.

She'd decided to go back to her car and do just that when Rick suddenly started the engine and drove off. She raced back to her own car and, speeding out of the parking lot, pulled onto the highway. Fortunately, traffic was sparse.

Spotting Rick ahead, she eased up on the gas pedal and followed at a discreet distance.

She was beginning to wonder if the van hadn't been a figment of her imagination. Maybe her

mind had conjured up the whole thing just to give
her an excuse to follow Rick. It was possible.

She shifted her weight. Her legs were stiff and
her back ached. She was hungry and more than a
little tired. That was the least of her problems. She
was almost out of gas.

They drove for another fifteen minutes before
Rick's right signal light blinked and he turned into
a gas station.

Fortunately, there was another station ahead.
Pulling into the driveway, she stopped in front of
a row of pumps. She filled her tank, keeping a
watchful eye on the Blazer across the street.

She hoped Rick remembered her warning not to
use his credit cards.

Moments later, she waited on the side of the
road for him, sipping a soft drink and munching
chips purchased from a vending machine. There
was still no sign of the van.

It was almost midnight by the time they reached
Route 139. There was little traffic on the road, no
more than an occasional truck or motor home.

She let up on the gas pedal. Once Rick reached
the dirt road to the cabin she would have to fall
back even farther or risk him spotting her.

She didn't want him to know she had followed
him all the way from San Francisco. He was
bound to jump to all the wrong conclusions and
would try to talk her into staying. And if she
stayed, she would end up in his arms again, end
up in his bed.

It wouldn't take much. All she had to do was

look into those sexy eyes of his and she would be putty in his hands.

Somehow, she'd found the strength to resist him earlier, but just because she'd done it once didn't mean she could manage the feat a second time.

Indeed, it would be a whole lot better for both of them if he didn't even know she was in the vicinity.

The taillights of the Blazer disappeared. This meant Rick had made the final turn onto the dirt road leading to the cabin.

She drove past the turnoff, watching the road ahead and behind. She planned to wait for a few minutes before circling back. No other car was in sight, and as long as she kept her eye on the intersection, Rick should be safe.

Suddenly, a light-colored van came speeding out of nowhere and swerved toward her. Only quick action on her part saved her from being driven off the road. Slamming on her brakes to keep from plowing into a tree, she swung in a U and sped off in the opposite direction.

With her eye on the rearview mirror, she tried using her cell phone, without success. "Rats!" She tossed the phone down and concentrated on the road. Much to her relief, no lights appeared in her rear window.

She almost missed the turn leading to Rick's cabin. Braking, she backed up and swung onto the dirt road.

Driving faster than she would normally dare to drive on the rutted road, she banged her head twice on the roof of her car before slowing down. There was still no sign that she was being followed.

It took her nearly forty minutes before she saw the lights from the windows of Rick's cabin. Pulling up beside his Blazer, she parked and unholstered her gun, checking the ammo.

Rick opened the door just as she climbed out of the car. "Jack! Is that you?"

"Get back!" she yelled. She darted from the car to the porch, clearing the steps in a single leap. "Hurry."

She pushed him inside and slammed the door shut behind her, her trembling fingers working the locks.

"What the hell...?"

"Shhh." She flipped off the light switch. It was a dark moonless night and the room was pitch-black.

"Would you mind telling me what's going on?" His voice was hushed, but no less demanding.

"Someone followed you from San Francisco," she whispered back. "Someone in a tan van."

"Really? But...why?"

"That's what I want to know." Feeling her way in the dark, she checked the locks on the windows. "This same person tried to run me off the road."

"Run you..." He sounded shocked. "Jacquie, are you okay?" The concern in his voice almost shattered what precious little resolve remained. One more kind word from him and bam! She was putty!

"Yeah," she said brusquely. "I'm here, aren't I?"

"I don't like this. I'd never forgive myself if something happened to you."

Oh, hell. He was doing it again. "Hush, will you?" she growled. "I'm trying to concentrate."

He laid a hand on her shoulder. "Jacquie—"

His hand seemed to burn through her suit jacket all the way to her skin. "Jack," she corrected. She tried to sound adamant, but her body trembled and her heart pounded and she was having a hell of a time keeping herself from succumbing to the lazy seductiveness of his voice.

His hand closed around her wrist. Before she could utter a protest, he pulled her into his arms and crushed her against his body. "Jack!" He covered her mouth hungrily with his, and the forceful domination of his lips rendered her momentarily helpless.

It was concern for his safety rather than self-control that prevented her from returning his kiss with the same reckless abandon.

It took every bit of strength to push him away. Gasping for air, she put as much distance between them as possible. Clawing frantically in the darkness, she stumbled across the room.

At that moment she hated him for what he was capable of doing to her. "Don't ever do that again!"

"You wanted it just as much as I did," he said. "Why deny it?"

"I'm here to save your fool neck and that's the only reason I'm here." She moved the draperies aside to watch the road. Not a car, not a headlight broke the solid black void surrounding the cabin.

Rick moved to the window directly behind her, and his closeness set every nerve in her body on edge. She couldn't see him, but she could feel his heat, smell the tangy fragrance of his aftershave. What was worse, his kiss still lingered on her mouth, searing her lips with burning flames.

"I've had time to do a lot of thinking since I saw you in San Francisco. What you said about me being a workaholic. It's true."

She bit down on her lower lip, willing him to stop talking. Maybe then she could concentrate on saving his life.

"I tried to think of the possible reasons why I am the way I am," he continued, his voice low. "I thought if I could understand why work has come to be my entire focus, maybe I could do something about it."

He moved closer and she held her breath. *Please don't let him touch me.*

"I had a learning disability in grade school..." he continued, his voice close to her ear. "Only back then, they didn't call it a learning disability. They called it stupid.

"But I learned pretty early that if I worked my fool head off, I could keep up with the other kids. So I studied longer and harder than anyone else. It worked. I graduated from high school with honors and earned a full four-year scholarship."

"That's great, Rick. But what does any of this have to do with the two of us?"

"That's what I'm trying to tell you. Old habits

are hard to break. When I stop working, I feel like everyone else will pass me by. I feel if I let my guard down for even a minute, I'll never be able to catch up."

"That might have been true when you were in grammar school, but it's not true now. Look how successful you are. Obviously, you've overcome your learning disability."

"Yeah, I have. But I still can't shake the feeling that I've got to work harder than anyone else. It's crazy, I know, but that's the reality."

"I'm sorry, Rick. I don't know what to say."

"I'm not telling you this because I want your pity. Hell, it took me years to understand why I'm the way I am. I can't expect you to understand."

She tightened her hands around her upper arms. "I think I do understand." She spoke slowly, because it suddenly occurred to her why her father was the way he was.

The youngest of eleven children born to Irish immigrants, he often told stories of coming to this country at the age of nine. Feeling like an outsider, he had worked like a dog to lose the Irish brogue that had made him a target of ridicule from the neighborhood kids. Maybe her father had similar fears of letting down his guard, of having to work longer and harder than anyone else just to stay afloat.

Feeling bone weary and confused, she glanced outside again. "It's late. And you said it yourself—you're behind in your work. You better get some rest so you can get an early start in the morning. I'll keep watch."

"We'll take turns. You take the first shift. I'll take the second."

"It's my job," she said.

"But—"

"Your work is important to you!" she snapped. "Why can't you accept the fact that my work is important, too? Like it or not, I'm your bodyguard, at least for tonight."

Silence followed her outburst, and for several long moments she didn't dare move for fear of bumping into him.

Finally, he moved away, and the scraping sound of a chair on the far side of the room told her she was no longer in imminent danger of being pulled into his arms.

"Good night!" His curt voice was like a knife slicing through the darkness. He stumbled over something on the way to the bedroom and she heard him curse beneath his breath. The slamming of his bedroom door provided the final barrier between them.

Holding on to the draperies with a tightly clenched hand, she thought she saw a fuzzy light in the distance. She blinked away the tears, but the light had disappeared. It was almost pitch-black outside, with only a few dim stars overhead to break the dark void.

Still, she was on edge. Someone was out there, watching as she was watching. Waiting as she was waiting. She could feel it.

18

THE ROSY GLOW OF DAWN spilled across the sky, setting the pointed tips of the shimmering pines afire with golden beams of sunlight. Closer to ground, early morning mist floated in the air like a dancer's discarded veils.

Jacquie stretched her arms overhead, then touched her toes, her body stiff. What she needed was a cup of her aunt's high-test coffee. Since that wasn't possible, she walked into the kitchen and made a pot with twice the necessary coffee grounds.

She had just poured herself a cup of pure caffeine when Rick joined her, dressed in blue jeans and a sweatshirt. His hair, damp from his shower, spilled onto his forehead, giving him a boyish look that tugged at her heartstrings.

"That smells good," he said. He reached over her head for a clean coffee mug, the scent of his freshly showered body causing a myriad of sensations to whirl inside her.

He poured himself a cup of coffee and she stared at his hands. It was amazing how hands that large could be so gentle. And they had been gentle the night he'd made love to her, touched her, searching for all her pleasures spots and finding even the ones she never knew existed.

Tearing her gaze away from him, she dropped a piece of rye bread into the toaster. "We need to go to town," she said. "I want to call Harrison. I don't have a license number for the van, but I can give him a description."

"I've got work to do," Rick said.

Her temper flared. "If that bomber gets his hands on you, you're never going to work again!"

His jaw tightened. "All right! I'll go to town with you. If that's what you want!"

"What I want is for you to find another place to stay. Somewhere with a telephone and a proper security system."

He sipped his coffee, watching her over the brim of his mug. Finally, he set the half-empty mug on the counter. "I'll pack my stuff."

The toast popped up, but she had suddenly lost her appetite. "I'll be waiting."

While Rick packed, Jacquie checked outside. As far as she could tell, there wasn't a single soul around. Nevertheless, she wasn't about to take chances. Walking slowly, cautiously, her senses alert, she followed a trail around the cabin, gun in hand. Then she saw it, hidden among the trees in the distance. The van.

Determined not to panic, she backtracked. She didn't want the owner of the van to know she'd spotted him. Her first instinct was to sneak up on the suspect and demand to know what he was doing there. But a bodyguard's duty was to protect a client, not apprehend a criminal.

She reached the cabin just as Rick walked outside, carrying a suitcase. Thinking quickly, she said the first thing that came to mind. "I've been thinking over what you said last night."

The hard expression on Rick's face softened. "I was hoping you would. Oh, Jack. Jacquie...does this mean you're willing to give us a second chance?"

She was tempted. He'd never know how much. "We'll talk inside."

To her relief, he turned and walked back into the cabin. She glanced around quickly, trying not to look obvious, before following him.

She slammed the door shut and bolted it. "He's out there!"

Rick's eyes clung to hers. "Are you sure?"

"I saw his car."

She jumped at the sound of breaking glass. Acting purely out of instinct, she threw herself in front of Rick, hand on her weapon. Something was on the floor by the fireplace. Smoke began to fill the room. Tear gas.

"Hurry!" Rick said. "This way." He grabbed her by the hand and pulled her across the room to the bedroom. Rick slammed the door and Jacquie ripped the quilted spread off the bed, stuffing it into the crack beneath the door.

Meanwhile, Rick pounded against the frame of the window with the palm of his hand. The frame was warped, but he was finally able to work it free.

"Wait!" She rushed to his side and glanced outside. They couldn't reach the car, but maybe they could escape through the woods. "I'll go first."

"No." He reached for her arm, but she pushed him away.

"It's my job," she said firmly. She climbed onto the windowsill and jumped the short distance to the ground. Gun ready, she glanced around.

Rick didn't wait for her to give him the all-clear sign. He scrambled over the window ledge and slid to the ground by her side. He held his arm out to her in a protective gesture that was as endearing as it was irritating.

For a split second, it was a question of which of them was doing the protecting.

Jacquie immediately asserted authority, as she had been trained to do. "Those trees," she said. "Go!"

Rick grabbed her by the hand and they raced across the clearing to the trees.

Whoever threw that tear gas into the house wanted them outside. He probably expected them to run toward the car. By the time he realized they had run in the opposite direction, they'd have gained a few precious moments' head start. It wasn't much, but it was something.

Winded, they reached the woods, but before Jacquie had time to catch her breath, a stranger stepped out from behind a tree, holding a gun.

Jacquie froze, but Rick surprised her by greeting the man with a friendly wave of his hand. "You're a sight for sore eyes. We're in trouble."

Jacquie kept her eyes on the man's face. "You know him?"

The man held his gun steady, his arm outstretched. "Yeah, he knows me. Now drop your gun, little lady. Drop it!"

Frowning, Rick shook his head. "It's okay, Lenny. Jack is my bodyguard. Jack, meet Leonard. He and I have been friends since grammar school." The lines on his forehead grew deeper. "Lenny? What are you doing with that gun?"

"I've come to claim my rightful place in the world," Lenny replied, his voice strangely monotone, almost singsong. "Now I mean it, lady, drop your gun."

Rick's face crumbled into a combination of shock and disbelief, and he turned a ghostly white. Jacquie felt sorry for him, but her main concern at the moment was to save her client, not offer comfort.

Lenny laughed, but there was nothing mirthful or even pleasant about it. "All my life," he said slowly, addressing his comments to Jacquie, "it's always been the same. Rick was the golden boy. The one who could do no wrong. He was always smarter and wiser than the rest of us. When I landed a job at Stanwicke and Lanswell, I thought I could finally prove myself."

Lenny swiped at a big yellow-and-black bee hovering around his head. "Then Rick started working there, too, and nothing was ever the same. Once again, he was the golden boy. The one everyone looked up to."

"That's not true, Leonard," Rick said, his words oddly disjointed, as if he was having trouble believing anything that was happening. "You're a talented man. A valued employee. Everyone knows that."

"I was. Until you came up with the idea for this new program that will revolutionize the entire computer industry. Nothing I do could possibly measure up to that. You know it as well as I do. Nothing!"

Rick shook his head in disbelief. "So you sent me a bomb?"

"Yeah, that was me. Pretty clever, huh? I sent a bomb to your office. You weren't supposed to be there that day, remember? You told me you were going to work at home. I planned for it to go off while the office was empty. Destroy your files and notes. Put you even more behind schedule. It was my insurance."

"Lenny, this is crazy. What did you hope to gain? You know I'm not going to give up."

"I needed time. Other people are working on the same idea. All the big companies. I wanted to give them time to come out with their product first. That would have stolen the thunder away from you. That would have ended your reign as the golden boy."

The pieces all began to fall into place and Jacquie felt sick. "You put Rick's life at risk just so he wouldn't get the credit for his work?"

"It would have been so simple had he taken a hint." Lenny stared at Rick, his eyes unnaturally bright. "But no, you persisted. No matter how many obstacles I put in your way, you kept making progress."

Rick's jaw tightened. "You mean you're responsible for all the problems I've had this last year?"

Again Leonard laughed, a cold, chilling, hollow sound that brought a shiver to Jacquie's spine. "Guilty as charged. I even arranged for that little bout of food poisoning."

The smile abruptly left Lenny's face. "Then you disappeared and I wasn't able to find you. I knew you were up here somewhere, but I couldn't find the cabin. Then yesterday, you called the boss and told him you were going to make your deadline. It was mighty considerate of you to tell Parker you were heading for the Spade Insurance Agency. From there, I was able to follow you."

Rick looked dazed, as if he had just woken from a nightmare. "We've been friends since we were kids. Surely that means something."

Leonard waved the gun in Rick's face. "You were never my friend. I was just someone who made you look good. You even beat me out of that scholarship."

"Lenny, I swear to God, I never meant to beat you out of anything—"

"Shut up! Put your hands over your head, both of you. And start walking. I think a little drowning accident is in order. Then you'll never be the golden boy again."

Rick tried to reason with Leonard. Though it was obvious the man was beyond reason, Jacquie was grateful to Rick for trying.

Just keep him busy, she pleaded silently. *Who knows? I might even figure out a way to get us out of this mess.*

Boot camp had taught her to avoid such situations, but had offered little in the way of practical advice on how to get out of them. Like it or not, she was on her own.

She scanned the area for something—anything—that might be useful. What she needed was more time. Time to do what, she had no idea, but time nonetheless. Given enough time, anything was possible, wasn't it?

A short distance ahead, a fallen log blocked the path. She glanced at the gunman, who was still arguing with Rick. *Okay, here goes nothing.* She timed her fall perfectly, landing on the ground with a bit more gusto than she intended.

Rick started toward her, but Leonard held him at bay. "Stay where you are."

Leonard stuck the barrel of his gun into her back. "Get up."

"I can't." She grimaced and reached for her leg. Recalling the times her high school drama coach had accused her of overacting, she decided against turning on the waterworks. "I think it's broken."

"Dammit, I said get up!"

"All right, if you insist." She rose to her knees slowly, groaning aloud. All right, so maybe she was overdoing it, but desperate times called for desperate measures.

"Shut up!" Leonard lifted his foot to kick her. Before he made contact, she grabbed his leg, catching him by surprise, and flipped him onto his backside.

Rick jumped him and the two men rolled in the dirt and struggled for the gun.

Leaping up, Jacquie searched for something to use as a weapon and spotted an oar in the tall grass by the water's edge; it had probably washed ashore after their boat overturned.

She picked up the oar just as Leonard staggered to his feet. He pointed his gun at Rick, his finger on the trigger. "Get up!"

Rick rose to his feet slowly, rubbing his chin.

Holding the oar over her shoulder like a baseball bat, she swung with all her might, hitting Leonard on the back of the head. Had it been a baseball, she would have scored a home run. Instead, Leonard fell to the ground, unconscious.

"We did it, Rick. We did it!" She swung around excitedly, inadvertently striking Rick on the side of the head with the oar.

Her eyes round in horror, she watched helplessly as Rick crumbled to the ground next to Lenny.

19

"RICK. SAY SOMETHING." Jacquie leaned over his hospital bed and shook him gently. So much had happened in the past twenty-four hours.

Mark had reported Jacquie's panicked phone call to Aunt Samantha, who immediately got on the phone to Tiny Tim and ordered him back to Falcon Heights to find out what the hell was going on.

Tiny Tim arrived just in time to tie up Leonard and carry Rick to the Blazer. Jacquie drove him to the hospital in record time, pleading with Rick all the way to open his eyes and say something.

Rick never stirred.

Jacquie stayed by his bedside all night long, waiting for him to regain consciousness and praying nothing was too drastically wrong with him. That's all she wanted. That and his forgiveness for nearly killing him a fourth time.

The doctor said he had a concussion, but the swelling appeared to be going down and that was a good sign.

It was nearly noon that second day before Rick gained consciousness. While the doctors checked him out, Jacquie paced outside his door. Finally, the medical team left and she slipped into his room.

"Jack?"

It was the first word he'd spoken since she'd knocked him out, and his rough, groggy voice was music to her ears.

She lowered herself to the chair next to his bed and leaned forward. "Thank God you're okay. How do you feel?"

"Like someone bashed me over the head." He tried sitting up.

"Here." She went to push the button that adjusted the bed, but nothing happened. "The bed isn't working," she said, plumping up the pillows behind his back.

"That's better." He gazed at her. "What happened? What am I doing here? Where's Lenny?"

"Whoa there. One question at a time. Leonard's where he belongs. In jail."

"I can't... The last thing I remember is seeing him on the ground."

"Yeah, well, we had a little accident."

"Accident?" He turned white and quickly glanced beneath the covers. "Don't tell me Lord Byron and I have something in common?"

"Don't be ridiculous." She bit her lip and glanced away.

"So what happened, Jack? What kind of accident?"

She tilted her head toward him. "All right, if you have to know. I kind of knocked you unconscious."

"Kind of?" He put his hand on the black-and-blue lump at his temple and groaned. "You mean Leonard didn't do this?"

"Rick, I'm sorry. I promise I'll never hurt you again. I'm going to tell my aunt that our deal is off. I'm a terrible bodyguard. I'm through trying to be something I'm not just to please my family."

"Thank God. I don't think I can survive one more day of your lifesaving methods." His eyes softened and she caught a glimpse of warm humor in their depths. After everything that had happened, he obviously still cared for her.

He squeezed her hand and pulled her onto the bed. Cupping her face, he kissed her, his lips nuzzling her mouth tenderly.

Reluctantly, she pulled back. It didn't seem like the right time for serious talk, but she was afraid that if she didn't say what she had to, she would surely burst. "Rick…I'm so sorry for all the trouble I've caused you."

"Trouble? What trouble? Oh, you mean the four times you've tried to kill me? Think nothing of it."

She smiled through her tears. "I'm serious, Rick. I've made some really bad choices these last few years. I went after a law degree I loathed, hoping to gain my father's attention. I agreed to work for my aunt because I thought it would please her. I've done all these things for the wrong reasons and nothing's worked out. If I get involved with a man, I have to know it's right."

His expression grew serious. "And you don't think I'm the right man?"

"What I'm trying to say..." She took a deep breath. "You're a workaholic and I hate that. But I hate the alternative even worse."

He looked confused. "The alternative?"

"I hate thinking of having to spend the rest of my life without you. I guess what I'm really saying is I love you just the way you are. I'm not going to try and change you, Rick."

He studied her long and hard. "You've said your piece. Do I get to say mine?"

She reached for a tissue and wiped her eyes. "Nothing you say can make me change my mind. You're stuck with me, Rick Westley."

"Then you really do need to hear what I have to say. Before you came in, I lay here thinking about Lenny. All these years..." Rick shook his head as if he couldn't believe that Lenny had turned against him. "I was so intent upon proving myself, it never occurred to me what I was doing to Lenny."

"You can't take responsibility for Leonard's shortcomings."

"But I do. Had I not been so damn determined to overcome my own inadequacies, I might have been a better friend to Lenny. Shown him how much I appreciated him as a person. Had he been made aware of his own talents, he might not have thought we were in competition with each other."

Rick touched a nerve inside. All these years, Jacquie had been so busy trying to compete with her family, she'd never considered her own worth. Maybe if she had accepted her own God-given talents and limitations, she would have more readily accepted her father's.

"We can both learn from Leonard's mistakes," she said.

Rick gazed at her with such softness in his eyes, it was like watching a sunset, a meteor shower and a rainbow all rolled into one. "Lenny had so much going for him. He has a wonderful wife and a great kid. Now that I look back, I realize he threw it all away, and for what? For a job!"

"He's not the first person to make that mistake," she said.

"No, he's not. The sad thing is, I've been missing out on life and I didn't even know it." Rick spoke slowly, as if it was important to get each word right. "Not until you and I went boating."

The mention of that day in the boat brought a blush to her face. It had been the happiest day of her life. At least, until the boat overturned.

"Hell, I never saw a meteor shower until you showed me one. And do you know what I did when I was driving back to the cabin after seeing you in San Francisco? I actually pulled the car over to the side of the road to watch the sunset."

Her mouth dropped open. So *that's* why he had stopped. To watch a sunset. She felt a wondrous joy inside. A sunset!

"I have to say, your bodyguard methods are a bit on the drastic side." He laughed.

She laughed, too, but only to keep her tears at bay.

"But," he continued, "there're other ways to

save someone. And you've saved me from a dull, boring existence. You're my saving grace, Jack. You said you wouldn't try to change me, but I want to change. I want to be the man you deserve, the man who loves you like you've never been loved in your life."

"Oh, Rick..." She was so touched by his words, she could hardly speak.

"I love you," he continued. "I think I loved you the moment I first set eyes on you."

"I love you." She wanted to say she, too, had loved him from the first moment they'd met, but that didn't seem right; somehow she felt as if she'd loved him all her life.

He reached out to her and she stared down at his hand before taking it in her own and holding it next to her cheek. Could a man like him really change? Could she? Maybe not. But it no longer mattered to her. All she cared about was the love they felt for each other.

Rick's doctor walked into the room, a Dr. Whittaker. "How are we feeling?"

Rick never took his eyes off Jacquie's face. "We've never felt better."

"Let's have a look," Dr. Whittaker said.

"I'll wait outside." Jacquie squeezed Rick's hand and walked out of his room. She had a lot to think about. Something wonderful had happened to her and she no longer felt burdened by the past. She loved Rick, yes, even the part of him she'd never thought she *could* love, and this was a wonderful, wonderful feeling.

Spotting a row of telephones at the end of the corridor, she suddenly had the urge to share her good news. She started toward them, digging into her tote bag for change.

She dialed the number of her father's office. "Janet, it's Jacquie. Is my father there?"

"I'm sorry, Jacquie. He had to be in court early today. Do you want me to leave a message?"

"No...yes." She bit her lip. Something suddenly occurred to her. All these years, she had resented her father for trying to turn her into something she wasn't.

She had done everything in her power to earn her father's approval, to no avail. For the first time she realized that perhaps she had gone about it all wrong. Maybe they both had. Instead of trying to change each other, maybe they needed only to accept each other.

"Jacquie?" Janet prompted. "Are you still there?"

"Yeah, I'm still here. Tell my father...I love him." She was amazed at how easy it was to say those three little words now that she had finally learned the meaning of unconditional love. She hung up the phone, feeling as if a heavy load had been lifted from her shoulders.

Rick was talking on the phone when she returned to his room. After another moment or so, he hung up. Reaching for her hand, he pulled her to the bed.

"I just called my boss and told him I intend to take a month-long vacation."

Her eyes widened in surprise. "You...are?"

"I thought it was time I caught up on all the things I've been missing out on. I haven't been to the beach since high school."

She shook her head in disbelief. "And you live in California."

"Unbelievable, isn't it? And Disneyland. I think I was last there when I was ten. I hear they have some new rides."

She laughed. "A few."

"And boating...I definitely want to do more boating." He thought a moment. "But this time let's do it in warmer waters."

He continued to cite an amazing and exhausting list of activities he wanted them to do together during his time off.

She laughed in delight. Only a workaholic would try to cram so much activity into a single vacation. "Oh, Rick. Do you really think you can spend a whole month doing *nothing?*" She was teasing him, of course, but he obviously missed the point.

"What do you mean, nothing? I just told you what we are going to do. I'm going to spend every moment proving to you just how much I love you."

"I love you, too," she whispered, and she meant that with all her heart. Even if he did drive her crazy at times.

He stared at her for the longest while, as if to memorize the way she looked at that moment.

"I'm going to prove I'm a changed man in a month's time. What do you say, Jack? Is it a deal?"

"Jacquie," she whispered. "Call me Jacquie." Jack had stopped existing the moment Rick had told her he loved her.

"Jacquie," he whispered back.

"What happens at the end of the month?" she asked, still unable to fully believe everything that had happened.

"If I so much as mention work, you're free to walk away at any time. If by some good fortune you're still with me at the end of the month, I shall propose marriage and hope you have the good sense to say yes."

"Oh, Rick." She held his hand to her face and pressed her lips into his palm. She already knew what her answer would be, and it didn't matter how the month turned out. "This next month is going to be perfect."

"Yeah, it will be." He ran a knuckle up her damp cheek. "I intend to make love to you every day, twice a day. On the beach. Beneath the stars." He leaned over and whispered in her ear one particular thing he intended to do to her.

Jacquie's face turned red. She drew back, flustered. "Oh, Rick!"

"Is that a yes?" he asked.

"Yes," she said. "Yes!" She leaned forward, meaning to kiss him on the lips. Instead, she inadvertently pressed the faulty button on the hospital bed.

This time, the button engaged and the top half

of the bed sprang up faster than lightning, sending Rick flying forward.

Lucky for *him* he ended up in her waiting arms. Lucky for *her*.

Jacquie looked so horrified at the thought of what could have happened had she not stopped his fall, he couldn't resist teasing her. "That's five."

Don't miss Temptation's next...
Hero for Hire

#709 A PRIVATE EYEFUL
Ruth Jean Dale

When Samantha Spade summoned Nicholas
Charles to a luxury desert resort he knew this
assignment would be different. For one thing,
none of the agents at S. J. Spade had ever met
their boss, for another she refused to tell him
what the assignment was, which left him
wondering what to do with his time...until he
met the delectable, enigmatic Corinne Leblanc.

Available in December
Here's a preview!

THE SEXY CADENCE of a woman's spike heels on hard wooden floors sent an expectant shiver through the waiting man. The rhythmic sound ceased abruptly just beyond the closed office door, to be replaced by an indistinct murmur of voices.

Ignoring a slight tensing of his shoulders, Nicholas Charles continued to stare out the third floor window at a fabulous view of the Golden Gate Bridge and San Francisco Bay. He knew what that sound meant; Samantha Joan Spade had arrived. After nearly four years in the employ of the S. J. Spade Insurance Agency—insurance in quotes, he was about to come face-to-face with his boss for the very first time.

To call her insistence on keeping a low profile eccentric would be an understatement. Although he'd spoken to her a few times on the telephone, routinely he'd been handed his assignments by her office staff, without ever coming face-to-face with the boss lady herself.

All that was now about to change. Keeping his breathing light and steady, he told himself he was ready for anything. He hoped it was true, but he had a funny feeling it might not be.

The truth was, Nick knew almost nothing about the mysterious S. J. Spade beyond the obvious:

that her insurance agency was really a front to protect the privacy of her personal protection clientele. Casual pumping and prying of her office staff had gotten him very little beyond the obvious—that she'd inherited the agency from a deceased husband who'd been a private detective, that she had no children, no pets, no known vices or addictions that anyone knew of and that she was damned good at what she did, provide peerless personal protection, for a price.

After a while, Nick had stopped asking. Then he got "The Call."

The Call came less than an hour after he'd safely delivered the wife of an international industrialist to a secret location in London, where her grateful husband waited anxiously. Nick had provided "insurance" for the terrified middle-aged woman, which included snatching her from beneath the noses of a gang of kidnappers, then hiding out with her in a cabin in the Adirondacks until the time was right for a white-knuckle dash to Kennedy Airport and an equally nerve-racking flight across the Atlantic.

It had been his third assignment in a row without more than a couple of days off in between. He figured he'd earned a nice, long vacation, and he'd been all set to take it—until the telephone in his hotel room rang mere minutes after he walked in.

"She wants to see you," Mark Spenser, Ms. Spade's San Francisco liaison, had announced after the obligatory congratulations-on-a-job-well-done.

"You mean in person?"

"That's right."

Nick felt a spark of interest which quickly died. He was too damned tired to care much. "When?"

"Yesterday." Mark sounded cheerful, as if he was enjoying this a shade too much. "I've already booked your flight out of Heathrow. You leave at five-fifteen."

"Not a chance. I couldn't get to the airport in time, even if I left now."

"Not to worry. Ms. Spade has friends in unexpected places. We've arranged an escort—"

"But until an hour ago, you didn't even know this job was finished."

"—should be arriving just about—"

Now, announced by a firm knock on the hotel door. A London bobby stood there, smiling and polite. Nick surrendered himself into the hands of the British law without the faintest idea how it had been accomplished.

Now that he had safely arrived in the boss's office with a bad case of jet lag compounded by mental exhaustion, he struggled to keep focused. In a battle of wits, he knew he was only half-armed at this moment. He also knew instinctively that it would take everything he had to deal with the hitherto elusive Samantha Spade.

HARLEQUIN
Temptation

He's strong. He's sexy. He's up for grabs!

Harlequin Temptation and
Texas Men magazine present:

1998 Mail Order Men

#691 THE LONE WOLF
by Sandy Steen—July 1998

#695 SINGLE IN THE SADDLE
by Vicki Lewis Thompson—August 1998

#699 SINGLE SHERIFF SEEKS...
by Jo Leigh—September 1998

#703 STILL HITCHED, COWBOY
by Leandra Logan—October 1998

#707 TALL, DARK AND RECKLESS
by Lyn Ellis—November 1998

#711 MR. DECEMBER
by Heather MacAllister—December 1998

*Mail Order Men—
Satisfaction Guaranteed!*

Available wherever Harlequin books are sold.

HARLEQUIN®
Makes any time special ™

MEN at WORK

All work and no play?
Not these men!

October 1998
SOUND OF SUMMER by Annette Broadrick

Secret agent Adam Conroy's seductive gaze could hypnotize a woman's heart. But it was Selena Stanford's body that needed saving—when she stumbled into the middle of an espionage ring and forced Adam out of hiding....

November 1998
GLASS HOUSES by Anne Stuart

Billionaire Michael Dubrovnik never lost a negotiation—until Laura de Kelsey Winston changed the boardroom rules. He might acquire her business...but a kiss would cost him his heart....

December 1998
FIT TO BE TIED by Joan Johnston

Matthew Benson had a way with words and women—but he refused to be tied down. Could Jennifer Smith get him to retract his scathing review of her art by trying another tactic: tying him *up*?

Available at your favorite retail outlet!

MEN AT WORK™

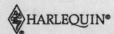 HARLEQUIN®  Silhouette®

Look us up on-line at: http://www.romance.net   PMAW3

COMING NEXT MONTH

#709 A PRIVATE EYEFUL Ruth Jean Dale
Hero for Hire
None of Samantha Spade's team of bodyguards had *ever* met their boss, so when she summoned Nicholas Charles, he was intrigued. And then annoyed. His assignment was to sit poolside in a luxury resort, waiting for something to happen. What happened was Corinne Leblanc—a prime suspect for *something*, with a body that demanded his undivided attention....

#710 THE REBEL'S RETURN Gina Wilkins
Southern Scandals
The prodigal son has come home for Christmas.... Fifteen years ago, young hell-raiser Lucas McBride was run out of town, accused of a crime he didn't commit. Now he's back to settle the score—and reclaim the girl he'd made a woman.

#711 MR. DECEMBER Heather MacAllister
Mail Order Men
Lexi Jordan only wants one thing for Christmas: a man! And who better than sexy Spencer Price, *Texas Men's* Mr. December himself. But one look at the gorgeous scientist has Lexi making a different kind of wish list—one that keeps Spencer in her bed well into the New Year....

#712 THE RIGHT MAN IN MONTANA Kristine Rolofson
Boots & Booties
Help wanted: Wife. When Sylvie Smith read the want ad, she was desperate. So she applied to a very sexy but *very* confused cowboy. It turned out that Joe Brockett's orphaned nieces and nephew had concocted this scheme to find a mommy for Christmas. But Sylvie couldn't stop thinking how great it would be to welcome Christmas morning as this man's wife....